Scarlet Wilson wrote her first story aged eight and has never stopped. She's worked in the health service for twenty years, having trained as a nurse and a health visitor. Scarlet now works in public health and lives on the West Coast of Scotland with her fiancé and their two sons. Writing medical romances and contemporary romances is a dream come true for her.

Also by Scarlet Wilson

One Kiss in Tokyo...
A Royal Baby for Christmas
The Doctor and the Princess
The Mysterious Italian Houseguest
A Family Made at Christmas
The Italian Billionaire's New Year Bride
Resisting the Single Dad
Locked Down with the Army Doc
Cinderella's New York Christmas
Island Doctor to Royal Bride?

Discover more at millsandboon.co.uk.

TEMPTED
BY THE HOT
HIGHLAND DOC

SCARLET WILSON

MILLS & BOON

First published in Great Britain 2019
by Mills & Boon, an imprint of HarperCollins*Publishers*
1 London Bridge Street, London, SE1 9GF

Large Print edition 2019

© 2019 Scarlet Wilson

ISBN: 978-0-263-07854-1

This book is produced from independently certified FSC™ paper to ensure responsible forest management. For more information visit www.harpercollins.co.uk/green.

Printed and bound in Great Britain
by CPI Group (UK) Ltd, Croydon, CR0 4YY

To my fab editor Carly Byrne,
for supporting me
to write the stories I love—
no matter how crazy!

PROLOGUE

'ABSOLUTELY NO WAY. I'm not doing it.' Kristie Nelson shook her head and folded her arms across her chest.

Louie, her boss, arched one eyebrow at her. 'Do you want to pay your mortgage or not?'

She shifted uncomfortably on her chair. 'I was promised a chance at working with the news team. These puff pieces are driving me nuts, and if you send me in the direction of another quiz show I swear I'll grab that ceremonial sword from behind your head and stick it somewhere nasty.'

Louie let out a hearty laugh. They'd been working together far too long to be anything but straight with each other.

He sighed and leaned his head on one hand. 'Kristie, your last two projects have bombed. You fell out—in a spectacular fashion, I might add—with the producer on the TV series you were scheduled for. I've had to search around for work that might fit with your other obligations.'

She swallowed, her throat instantly dry. Louie knew her well—better than most because she revealed nothing to most people—and, although she didn't tell him so, she did appreciate it.

She stared down at the file he'd handed her. '*A Year in the Life of the Hot Highland Doc*? Really?' Her voice arched upwards, along with her eyebrows. She tried to ignore the involuntary shudder that went down her spine. She straightened her shoulders. 'Sounds like another puff piece to me.'

Louie looked her in the eye. 'A puff piece that involves filming three days a month on the island—paid travel to and from the island, all expenses covered, and a salary better than any news channel would pay you.'

She shifted uncomfortably in her chair. When he put it like that…

Louie continued. 'These streaming TV channels are the ones with the big budgets these days. They're making all the best new TV shows, and they're not afraid to take chances.

Don't you think it might be a good idea to get in there, and make a good impression?'

Her brain was whirring. She knew it all made sense. She knew it was an opportunity. How many people really made it onto the terrestrial TV channels? She didn't even want to admit that she'd subscribed to this streaming service too. Some of the shows were addictive.

Louie shrugged. 'Filming is taking place all around the world. There's a volcanologist in Hawaii. A museum curator in Cairo. A quarterback from an American football team. Someone training for the space station.'

'And I get the Scottish doc?' She held up her file, not even trying to hide the disappointment on her face.

Louie didn't speak and the silence told her everything she needed to know. She'd got what was left. Louie had probably had to campaign hard to even get her this gig.

She flicked through the files sitting on Louie's desk. There was also a vet. A firefighter. A teacher. A policewoman.

If she'd had to rank each of the possibilities, she knew the work with the doc would have been last on her list. The thought of being around a medic all day—possibly being in a hospital environment—made her feel sick.

Six years ago as a media graduate she'd thought she was going to take the world by storm. But somehow that storm had changed into a long, hard slog with only a few glimmers scattered throughout. Part of her resented this job already. It wasn't exactly her career goal. But what was?

Things had shifted in the last few years. Real life events had left her jaded and knocked her confidence in the world around her. Sometimes she wasn't even sure what it was she was fighting for any more.

'Isn't describing someone as a Hot Highland Doc considered sexist these days?'

Louie shrugged. 'Who cares? That's the title we liked. It should draw viewers in. Who wouldn't want to see a Hot Highland Doc?'

Her brain was still ticking. She wrinkled her nose. 'Geography isn't my strong point. Hold on.' She pulled out her phone and stuck in the name of the island. 'Arran? That's on the southwest coast of Scotland. That's not even in the Highlands.'

Louie laughed. 'Like I said—who cares? At

least it is an island. It's the UK, so trade descriptions can't get us on that one.'

Kristie closed her eyes for a second and thought about the pile of bills currently sitting on her dresser. This was money. Money that would be guaranteed for one year. She would be a fool to turn this down.

'Smile. Arran—who knows? You might even like it. You just need to go there three days a month and film as much as you can. You need enough footage for forty-one minutes of screen time.' Louie waved his hand. 'And if it's boring, do something to mix it up.'

This time it was Kristie that raised her eyebrows. 'Mix it up? What exactly does that mean?'

Louis shrugged. 'I mean, make it interesting viewing. If you work on another show that gets cancelled midway, people will start to think you have the kiss of death.' He met her gaze. 'People won't want to work with you.' He left the words hanging.

She gulped. She knew he was right. TV and media were ruthless. One minute you were the belle of the ball, the next you were lucky to pick up the leftovers—just like she was now.

She gave a slow nod of her head then frowned as she compared her file with some of the others. 'This guy? There's no photo.'

'Isn't there?' Louie had moved over to his appointment diary, obviously ready to move onto his next task.

'And how do you even say his name?'

Louie moved back around the desk and leaned over her shoulder. '"Roo-ah-ree", I think.' He winked. 'At least try and get the guy's name right.'

She stared at the scribbled notes in the folder. Rhuaridh Gillespie. General Practitioner. Also provides cover to Arran Community Hospital and A and E department.

How did that even work?

She swallowed and took a deep breath. How bad could this be?

'How much preparation time do I have?'

There was a glint in Louie's eyes as he threw something across the desk at her. Flight details.

'A day,' he answered.

'A day?' She stood up as she said the words. 'What do you mean, a day?'

Louie just started talking as if there was nothing unusual at all about what he'd just said. 'You fly into Glasgow, car hire has been arranged—you need to drive to a place called Ardrossan to catch the ferry to Arran. The crossing takes about an hour but…' he paused as he glanced at some notes in front of him '…apparently can be hampered by the weather. So build in some extra time.'

Her brain had gone directly into overdrive. Clothes. Equipment. What was the weather like on Arran this time of year? This was the UK, not the US. She needed to learn a bit more about their healthcare system. And what about this guy? Under normal circumstances she'd take a few days to do some background research on him—to learn what kind of a person he was—what made him tick. Anything that would give her a head start.

She shook her head. Then realised she hadn't asked one of the most important questions. 'Who is my cameraman?'

Louie gave a little cough that he tried to disguise as clearing his throat. 'Gerry.'

'Gerry?' She couldn't hide her dismay. 'Louie, he's about a hundred and five! He doesn't keep up well, his timekeeping is awful, and he always leaves half his equipment behind.'

Louie gave a half-hearted shrug. 'Give the guy a break. He needs the work. And anyway, he knows you better than most.'

She bit her lip as she picked up her bag. Maybe she was being unreasonable. He did know her better than most—he'd been there with her and Louie when she'd got that terrible call. But last time she'd worked with Gerry he'd left her sitting in the middle of a baking desert in Arizona for three hours.

'I swear if he isn't at the airport when I get there, I'm leaving without him.'

Louie waved his hand. 'Whatever.' Louie picked up his phone as she headed to the door. 'And, Kristie?'

She spun back around. 'Yeah?'

He grinned. 'Who knows—you might enjoy this.'

She didn't hesitate. She picked up a cushion from the chair nearest the door and launched it at Louie's head.

CHAPTER ONE

May

THERE WAS NO way that this amount of vomiting could be normal. Maybe it was something she'd eaten on the flight between Los Angeles and London? The chicken had looked okay. But then she'd had that really huge brownie at Heathrow Airport before the departure to Glasgow.

She groaned as her stomach lurched again and the roll of the waves threw her off balance. They weren't even out at sea any more, they were in the middle of docking at the harbour in Brodick, Arran.

'First-timer, eh?' said a woman with a well-worn face as she walked towards the gangway.

Kristie couldn't even answer.

Gerry gave her a nudge. 'Come on, they've already made two announcements telling drivers to get back into their cars. Do you want me to drive instead?'

She shook her head and took another glug of water from the bottle he'd bought her. Poor Gerry. He'd spent half of this ferry journey holding the hair from her face so she could be sick. He was more than double her age, but seemed to have weathered the journey much better than she had—even if he had twice tried to get into the car on the wrong side.

She gave him a half-hearted smile. 'Next time we get on a flight together I'll have what you're having.' He'd popped some kind of tablet as soon as they'd boarded the flight in Los Angeles and had slept until the wheels had set down at Heathrow.

He returned a smile. 'What can I say? Years of experience.'

She watched him shuffling down the stairs in front of her to the car deck. The boat's bow was already opening, preparing for the cars to unload. Kristie ignored a few pointed glares as she made her way to their hire car and tried to squeeze back inside.

The cars in front had already moved by the time she'd started the unfamiliar vehicle and tried to remember what to do with the pedals and the gearstick.

She jumped as there was a loud blast of a horn behind her. She muttered an expletive under her breath as she started the car and promptly stalled it. The car juddered and heat rushed into her cheeks. 'Why is everything on the wrong side?'

Gerry chuckled. 'Just watch out for the roundabouts.'

She bit her bottom lip as she started the car again. The roundabout at Glasgow airport had been like an episode of the *Wacky Races*. The whole wrong-side-of-the-road aspect had totally frazzled her brain and she was sure at one point her life had flashed before her eyes.

'Arran isn't that big,' she muttered. 'Maybe they don't need roundabouts. Crazy things anyway. Who invented them? What's wrong with straight roads?'

Gerry laughed as they finally rolled off the ferry and joined the queue of traffic heading towards a road junction.

'Which way?' she asked.

'Left,' he said quickly. 'The doctor's surgery

and hospital are in a place called Lamlash. It's only a few miles up the road.'

Gerry settled back in his seat as they pulled out onto the main road. The sun was low in the sky and all around them they could see green on one side and sea on the other.

'I think I'm going to like this place,' he said with a smile, folding his hands in his lap.

Kristie blinked. Although there were a number of people around the ferry terminal, as soon as they moved further away the crowds and traffic seemed to disperse quickly. There was a cluster of shops, pubs and a few hotels scattered along what appeared to be the main street of the Scottish town, but in a few moments the main street had disappeared, only to be replaced with a winding coastal country road.

'I've never seen so much green,' she said, trying to keep her eyes fixed on the road rather than the extensive scenery.

Gerry laughed. 'You don't get out of Los Angeles often enough. Too much dry air.'

A few splotches of rain landed on the windscreen. Kristie frowned and flicked a few of the levers at the side of the wheel, trying to locate the wipers. The blinkers on the hire car flicked on and off on either side. She let out a huff of exasperation as she tried the other side.

'Road!' Gerry's voice pulled her attention back to the road as an approaching car honked loudly at her. She yanked the wheel back in an instant, her heart in her mouth. The car had drifted a little into the middle of the road as she'd tried to find the wipers. She cursed out loud as she pulled it back to the correct side of the road—which felt like the wrong side. 'Darn it. Stupid road,' she muttered.

Gerry shook his head. 'No multiple lanes here. Get with it, Kristie. Embrace the country-side.'

She pressed her lips together. She hadn't seen a single coffee shop she recognised, or any big department stores. What did people do around here? Her grip tightened on the wheel as the rain changed from a few splats to torrential within a few seconds. Her hand flicked the lever up and then down to quicken the wind-screen-wiper speed. It was almost as if a black cloud had just drifted over the top of them. She leaned forward and tried to peer upwards. 'What is this? Five minutes ago the sun was shining.'

She knew she sounded cranky. But she was tired. She was jet-lagged. She wanted some decent coffee and some hotel room service. She didn't even know what time zone she was in any more.

A sign flashed past. 'What did that say?' she snapped.

'Go left,' said Gerry smoothly.

She flicked the indicator and pulled into the busy parking lot in front of her. There was a white building to their right, set next to the sea.

The rain battered off the windscreen and the trees edging the parking lot seemed to be lolling to one side in the strong winds.

Gerry let out a low laugh at her horrified face. 'Welcome to Scotland, Kristie.'

'Tell me you're joking.' He stared across the room at his colleague Magda, who had her feet up on a nearby stool and was rubbing her very pregnant belly. She sighed. 'I signed the contract ten months ago. Before, you know, I knew about this.'

'You signed a contract for filming in our practice without discussing it with me?'

She shot him an apologetic look. 'I did discuss it with you.' She leaned forward to her laptop and scrolled. 'There.' She pointed to her screen. 'Or maybe not quite discussed, but I sent you the email. I forwarded the details and the contracts. So much has happened since then.' She let her voice slow for a second.

He knew what she meant. In the last year he'd gone from helping out at the practice as a locum to taking over from his dad when he'd died. This had been his father's GP practice, and Rhuaridh had been left in the lurch when his father had been diagnosed with pancreatic cancer and died in the space of a few weeks. Due to the difficulties in failing to recruit to such a rural post, he'd spent the last ten months, giving up his own practice in one of the cities in Scotland, packing up his father's house and selling his own, and trying to learn the intricacies of his new role. It was no wonder this piece of crucial information hadn't really stuck.

He ran his hand through his thick hair. 'But what on earth does this mean?'

Magda held up her hands. 'I'm sorry. I meant to talk to you last week when I sent them your details instead of mine—but I had that scare and just didn't get a chance.'

Rhuaridh swallowed and took a look at Magda's slightly swollen ankles. This was a much-wanted baby after seven years of infertility. Last week Magda had had a small fall and started bleeding. It had been panic stations all round, even from the team of completely competent staff in this practice and at the nearby cottage hospital. It seemed that practically the whole island was waiting for the safe delivery of this baby. There was no way he was going to put his colleague under any strain.

He sighed and sat down in the chair in front of her as he ran his fingers through his hair. 'Tell me again about this.'

The edges of her lips quirked upwards. They both knew he was conceding that she hadn't really told him properly at all.

'It's a TV show. *A Year in the Life of...*' She held out her hands. 'This one, obviously, is a doctor. It's an American company and they specifically wanted a doctor from Scotland who worked on one of the islands.'

He narrowed his gaze. 'I didn't know you wanted to be a reality TV star.' He was curious, this didn't seem like Magda at all.

She laughed and shook her head. 'Reality

TV? No way. What I wanted, and what we'll get—' she emphasised the words carefully '—is a brand-new X-ray machine for the cottage hospital, with enough funds for a service contract.'

'What?' He straightened in the chair.

She nodded. 'It's part of the deal.'

Rhuaridh frowned. How had he managed to miss this? The X-ray machine in their cottage hospital was old and overused. Even though the staff had applied to the local health board every year for an upgrade and new facilities, NHS funding was limited. While their machine still worked—even though it was temperamental—it was unlikely to be replaced. A new machine could mean better imaging, which would lead to fewer referrals to the mainland for potential surgeries. Fractures could be notoriously hard to see. As could some chest complaints. A better machine would mean more accurate diagnosis for patients and less work all round.

He looked at Magda again with newfound admiration. 'This is the reason you applied in the first place, isn't it?'

She grinned and patted her belly again. 'Give a little, get a little. You know I hate reporting on dusky X-rays. We'll have a brand-new digital system where we can enlarge things, and ping them on to a specialist colleague if we need to.' She shrugged, 'Just think of all those ferry journeys that won't need to happen.'

He nodded. Being on an island always made things tougher. Their cottage hospital only had a few available beds, which were inevitably full of some of the older local residents with chronic conditions. They had a small A and E department and a fully equipped theatre for emergencies but it was rarely used. Occasionally a visiting surgeon would appear to carry out operations on a couple of patients at a time, but they weren't equipped to carry out any kind of major surgery and any visiting consultant had to bring their whole team.

Whilst their facilities were probably adequate for their population of five thousand, every year the influx of holiday tourists during the summer months took their numbers to over twenty thousand. Slips, trips and falls made the X-ray machine invaluable. Rhuaridh had lost count of the number of times he'd had to send someone with a questionable X-ray over on the ferry to the mainland for further assessment.

'Sometimes I think I love you, Magda,' he said as he shook his head.

She wagged her finger. 'Don't tell David you said that, and just remember that while I tell you the rest.' He smiled. He'd known Magda's husband for the last ten years. He'd watched his friend battle to win the heart of the woman in front of him.

'What's the rest?' he asked as he stood up and stretched his back.

Magda bit her bottom lip. 'The filming happens for three days every month. You don't have to do anything special. They just follow you about on your normal duties. They take care of patient consent for filming. You just have to be you.'

The words were said with throwaway confidence but from the look on Magda's face she knew what was coming.

'Three days every month?'

She nodded. 'That's all.'

He pressed his lips together. It didn't sound like *That's all* to him. It sounded like three days of someone following him around and annoying him constantly with questions. It sounded like three days of having to explain to every single patient that someone was filming around him. He could kiss goodbye to the ten-minute consultation system that kept the GP practice running smoothly. He could wave a fond fare-well to his speedy ward rounds in the com-munity hospital where he knew the medical history of most of the patients without even looking at their notes.

'Three days?' He couldn't keep the edge out of his voice. He'd spent his life guarding his privacy carefully. Magda knew this. They'd trained together for six years, then jokingly followed each other across Scotland for a va-riety of jobs. It had been Rhuaridh who had introduced Magda to the isle of Arran off the west coast of Scotland—a place she'd fallen instantly in love with. It had been Rhuaridh who had introduced Magda to his best friend David, and his father Joe, who'd looked after the cottage hospital and GP practice on the is-land for thirty years. She knew him better than most. She knew exactly how uncomfortable this would make him.

She put her feet on the floor and leaned forward as best as she could with her swol-len stomach. 'I know it's bad timing. I never thought this would happen.' Tears formed in the corners of her eyes. 'I always meant for it to be me that did the filming. I thought it might even be fun. Some of our oldies will love getting a moment on TV.'

He could hear the hopeful edge in her voice. He knew she was trying to make it sound better for him.

He shook his head. 'It…it'll be fine, Magda. Don't worry. You know I'll do it.' He could say the words out loud but he couldn't ignore the hollow feeling in his chest. Three days' filming every month for the next year. It was his equivalent of signing up for the ultimate torture. This was *so* not his comfort zone.

He took a deep breath. 'Okay, it's fine. You concentrate on baby Bruce. Don't worry about anything. We both know you should currently be at home, not here. Leave this with me.'

She gave a half-scowl. 'I am *not* calling my baby Bruce.'

It was a standing joke. David's family had a tradition of calling the firstborn in their family Bruce. David had missed out. He was the secondborn. Once Magda had got past the three-month mark both David and Rhuaridh had started teasing her about the family name.

He laughed. 'You know you are. Don't fight it.' He glanced at the pile of work sitting on his desk. It would take him until late into the night. With Magda going on maternity leave, and no locum doctor recruited to fill the gap, everything was going to fall to him. He was lucky. He worked within a dynamic team of advanced nurse practitioners, practice nurses and allied health professionals. He already knew they would support him as best they could.

Life had changed completely for him once his father had died. He'd felt obligated to come back and provide a health service for the people of the island when the post couldn't get filled. Unfortunately, Zoe, his partner, had been filled with horror at the thought of life on Arran. He hadn't even had the chance to ask whether she thought a long-distance relationship could work. She had been repelled by the very prospect of setting foot on the island he'd previously called home and had run, not walked, in the opposite direction.

All of that had messed with his head in a way he hadn't quite expected. He loved this place. Always had, always would. Of course, as a teenager wanting to study medicine, he'd had to leave. And that had been good for him. He'd loved his training in the Glasgow hospitals, then his time in Edinburgh, followed by a job in London, and a few months working for Doctors Without Borders, before taking up his GP training. But when things had happened and his father died suddenly? That whole journey home on the boat had been tinged with nostalgia. Coming home had felt exactly like coming home should. It had felt as if it was supposed to happen—even though the circumstances were never what he had wanted.

He moved over towards the desk and looked at Magda. 'So, when exactly does this start? In a few months?'

There was a nervous kind of laugh. 'Tomorrow,' Magda said as she stared out the window. 'Or today,' she added with a hint of panic as her eyes fixed on the woman with blonde hair blowing frantically around her face in the stiff Firth of Clyde winds. Rhuaridh's eyes widened and he dropped the file he'd just picked up.

'What?' His head turned and followed Magda's gaze to the car park just outside his surgery window.

The woman was dressed in a thin jacket and capri pants. It was clear she was struggling with the door of her car as it buffeted off her body then slammed in the strong winds. She didn't look particularly happy.

'You've got to be joking—now? No preparation time, nothing?'

Magda gave an uncomfortable swallow, her blue eyes meeting his. 'Sorry,' she whispered. 'I just got caught up in other things.'

He could sense the panic emanating from her. He felt his annoyance bubble under the surface—but he'd never show it.

His brain started to whirl. He'd need to talk to patients. Set up appropriate consultations. Make sure nothing inappropriate was filmed. He wanted to run a few questions past his professional organisation. He knew there had been some other TV series that had featured docs and medical staff, and he just wanted a bit of general advice.

A piece of paper flew out of the hand of the woman outside. 'Darn it!' Even from inside her American accent was as clear as a bell.

Magda made a little choking sound. He turned to face her as she obviously tried to stifle her laugh. Her eyebrows rose. 'Well, she looks like fun.'

Rhuaridh pressed his lips together to stop himself from saying what he really wanted to say. He took another breath and wagged his finger at Magda. 'Dr Price, I think you owe me.'

She held out her hand so he could help pull her up from the chair. 'Absolutely.' She smiled.

Gerry seemed to be taking the wind in his stride. 'Why did we come here first?' she muttered as she opened the boot of the car to grab some of their equipment.

'Best to get things started on the right foot. Let's meet our guy, establish some ground rules, then crash.'

She gave him a sideways glance. Maybe her older colleague was more fatigued than he was admitting. She batted some of her hair out of her face. The sign outside the building read 'Cairn Medical Practice', with the names of the doctors underneath.

'Roo-ah-ree.' She practised the name on her tongue as they made their way to the main entrance. Gerry already had a camera under one arm. One thing for Gerry, he was ever hopeful.

'Roo-ah-ree.' She practised again, trying to pretend she wasn't nervous. So much was riding on this. She had to make it work. She had to make it interesting and watchable. There hadn't been background information on this doc. Apparently he'd been the last-minute replacement for someone else. And if he was anything like the majority of the people on the ferry he would be grey-haired, carry a walking stick, and be wearing a sturdy pair of boots.

The ferry. What if she still smelled of sick? She felt a tiny wave of panic and grabbed some perfume from her bag, squirting it madly around her before they went through the main entrance door.

They stepped into a large waiting area. It was empty but looked…busy. Some of the chairs were higgledy-piggledy, magazines and a few kids' toys were scattered around the tables and floor. She could see some tread marks on the carpet. This place had a well-used feel about it.

She glanced at her watch. There was no one at the reception desk. It was after six p.m. The sign on the door said that was closing time. 'Hello?' she ventured.

There was the slam of a door from somewhere and a tall ruffled, dark-haired man appeared from the back of the building. He had the oddest expression on his face. It looked almost pained.

'Hi, sorry,' he said. 'Just seeing my pregnant colleague out.' His eyes seemed to run up and down the two of them. 'You must be the TV people.'

His accent was thick, almost lilting, and it actually took her a few seconds to tune in and process his words. A frown appeared on his forehead at the delay. 'Rhuaridh Gillespie?' He lifted his hand and pointed to his chest.

Oh, my goodness. She was going to have to concentrate hard—and she didn't just mean because of the accent. He was so *not* what she expected. Instead of an old wrinkly guy, she had a lean, muscled guy with bright blue eyes and slightly too long tousled dark hair. He was wearing a light blue shirt and dress pants. And he didn't look entirely pleased to see them.

Something sparked in her brain and she walked forward, holding her hand out, knowing exactly how dishevelled she looked after their long journey. 'Kristie Nelson. It's a pleasure to meet you, Roo—' She stumbled a little. 'Dr Gillespie,' she said, praying that her signature smile would start working any moment soon.

For a while, that had kind of been her trademark. With her styled blonde locks, usually perfect makeup and 'signature' wide smile, there had been a time on local TV when she'd become almost popular. That had been the time she'd had oodles of confidence and thought her star was going to rise immensely and catapult her to fame and fortune. Instead, she'd fallen to the earth with a resounding bump.

He reached over and took her hand. It was a warm, solid grip. One that made her wonder if this guy worked out.

'Like I said, Rhuaridh Gillespie.' He leaned over and shook Gerry's hand too.

'Gerry Berkovich. Camera, lights, sounds and general dogsbody for the good-looking one.' He nodded towards Kristie.

She slapped his arm. 'As if!'

Dr Gillespie didn't even crack a smile. In fact, he barely held in his sigh. He gestured towards the nearest office. 'Come and have a seat. I've kind of been thrown in at the deep end here, so we're going to have to come to an agreement about some boundaries.'

It was the edge to his tone. She shot a glance at Gerry, who raised one corner of his eyebrow just a little. This didn't sound like the best start.

She swallowed and tried to ignore the fact she was tired, now hungry, and desperately wanted a shower and five minutes lying on a bed and staring up at a ceiling. She'd been travelling for twenty hours. She'd been in the company of other people for more than that. Sometimes she needed a bit of quiet—a bit of down time. And it didn't look like it would happen anytime soon.

Rhuaridh showed them to seats in his office.

Kristie had dealt with lots of difficult situations over the last few years in TV and moved into autopilot mode. 'I'm sure everything will be fine,' she said smoothly. 'Contracts have already been agreed—'

'Not by me,' he cut in sharply, 'And not by my patients. In fact...' he took a deep breath, lifting one hand and running it through his dark scraggy hair '... I'll need to get my professional organisation to take a look at this contract to make sure no patient confidentially will be breached inadvertently.'

He was speaking. But she wasn't really hearing. It was all just noise in her ears.

'This was all looked at—all prepared beforehand.' She could cut in too. As it went, she didn't know a single thing about the show's contracts because she'd had nothing to do with any of this. All she knew was she was on a schedule. She had three days to film enough stuff to get forty-one minutes of usable footage. Much harder than it sounded.

'I've been thrown into this. I won't do anything to compromise my patients, or my position here.' His voice was jagged and impenetrable. She could see him building a solid wall in front of himself before her very eyes. Her very tired eyes.

She'd thought he'd looked kind of sexy earlier. If this guy could do a bit of charm, the ladies would love him. But it seemed that charm and Dr Gillespie didn't go in the same sentence. 'I'm sure that—'

He stood up sharply. 'I won't move on this.'

'But we only have three days…'

Gerry gave a little cough. She turned sideways to look at him and he gave an almost invisible shake of his head.

'I'll get back to you as soon as I can. I suggest you go and check into your accommodation and try and…' he shot her a glance as if he was struggling to find the right words '…rest.'

He walked over to the door and opened it for them. This time he didn't even meet her gaze. 'I'll be in touch.'

Kristie was feeling kind of dazed. Had she just been dismissed? She wanted to stand and argue with him. Who did this guy think he was? Arrogant so-and-so. She'd travelled twenty hours for this.

But it was almost as if Gerry read her mind. He grabbed hold of her elbow as he led her back to the car.

The sky had got darker again as thick grey clouds swept overhead, followed by the obligatory spots of rain.

She opened the car and slumped into the driver's seat. Gerry started talking. 'I can shoot some of the scenery. Get a shot of the exteriors, the roads, the surgery. Maybe we could get someone to show us around the—what did they call it in the file—cottage hospital? I could even get a few shots of the ferry docking and leaving.'

'That will fill about five minutes of film when it's all edited down,' she groaned. She leaned forward and banged her head on the steering wheel. 'Why didn't I get the museum curator in Cairo? The person who is training to be an astronaut? Why did I have to get the grumpy Scottish doctor?' She thumped her head again, just to make sure Gerry understood just how frustrated she was.

'Kinda good looking, though,' he said unexpectedly.

'What?' She sat back up and shot him a weird look.

'I said, he's kind of good looking. And that cross demeanour? I think some folks might like it.'

Kristie shook her head. 'At this rate the whole first episode will have to be subtitled. Did you hear how fast he talks? And how thick that accent is?'

Gerry gave a slow appreciative nod as he folded his arms across his chest. 'He's practically got Highland warrior stamped on his forehead.' He twisted towards her and tapped one finger on his chin, looking thoughtful. 'Hey? What do you think your chances are of getting him in a kilt?'

It was no use. Her brain was clearly switching off, and Gerry's was clearly switching on. She just couldn't function.

She let out a kind of whimper. 'Blooming Arran. I need food, a shower and a bed. Tell me you know where our hotel is.'

Gerry smiled. 'It's about a five-minute drive from here. And it's not a hotel. It's a cottage. Apparently accommodation can be tricky here. There're only a few hotels, but some holiday lets. We'll be lucky if we stay in the same place twice.'

Kristie put both hands on the steering wheel and started the engine. 'Just tell me which direction.' Her head was starting to thump. It was probably the jet-lag and a bit of dehydration.

If she couldn't get something in the can in the next three days she would be toast. Her career was already dangling by a thread. Another failure against her name and Louie would be right—no one would want to work with her.

She was going to have to try all her Kristie charm on Dr Grump. Because if she didn't, who knew what could happen next?

They were sitting in his waiting room—again. Patients had already started asking questions. Some were even volunteering to be filmed. Three days of this every month for the next year?

He'd checked with his union. Apparently the TV contract was standard, and the appendix regarding patient consent was similar to one used by other TV series. As long as consent was granted and paperwork completed, there was no reason for him not to continue.

Truth was, he'd heard this news one day ago, but still couldn't bring himself to tell the TV crew. The guy—Gerry—permanently looked as if he could go to sleep at the drop of the hat, whereas his counterpart—Kristie—looked more wound up than the tightest spring.

Pam, one of the secretaries, stuck her head around the door. She had a sheaf of messages in her hand. 'Hospital called. X-ray problems again. Mrs McTaggart needs her painkillers upped. John Henderson phoned—sounded terrible—I've put him down for a house call, and…' She paused for a second, giving him a wary look. 'And I've got his permission to take the film crew.'

Rhuaridh's head flicked up from the bunch of prescriptions he'd been signing. Pam sighed. She was another member of staff that he'd inherited from his father, meaning she knew him better than most. 'You did what?'

Pam never pandered to him. 'Magda had already gone through all the patient permissions with me. So I've started getting them. Now hurry up and take that woman out of my waiting room before she spontaneously combusts.' Pam spun around and left, not giving him any chance to respond.

Rhuaridh leaned back in his chair and glanced at his watch. Nearly three p.m. He could do this. A few hours today, then all of tomorrow and he wouldn't have to see them again for another month. He tried to rationalise it in his brain. How bad could this be?

He pasted his best kind of smile on his face and walked outside.

Finally. He'd finally graced them with his presence.

There were only so many outdoor shots they could film on Arran—and Gerry had shot them all. Filler time, to use around the actual, proper filming. The thing they didn't have a single second of.

For a second yesterday, as they'd sat in the waiting room all day, she'd had half a mind to try and put a secret camera in this guy's room. It wasn't that she didn't know all the unethical issues with this, it was just that she was feeling *that* desperate.

And after two days of waiting, Rhuaridh Gillespie gave them a half-nod of his head. 'I've checked things out. We need to go to the local hospital. You'll need to sort out your permissions with the patients when you get there.'

She refused to let that make her mad. She'd already spent part of the night before meeting the nurse manager in charge at the hospital and sorting out all the paperwork with the long-stay patients.

She hadn't let Gerry see that she'd actually been sick outside before they'd entered. She'd been determined that she had to get the first visit to the place over and done with. Once they'd got inside and made the obligatory introductions she'd stuck her hands in her pockets so no one could see them shaking. If she'd had any other choice, she would have walked away from filming inside a hospital. But the fact was, there wasn't another choice. It was this, or nothing. So she'd pushed all her memories into a box and tried to lock it up tight.

Once the horrible squirming feeling in her stomach had finally disappeared, she'd decided that distraction was the best technique so she'd spent some time talking with some of the older patients, and had already decided to go back and interview a few of them on camera.

So by the time they joined Rhuaridh in his black four-by-four and he drove down the road to the hospital she felt a bit better prepared and that horrible ominous sensation had diminished a little. The journey only took a few minutes.

It became pretty clear in the first moments after they entered the hospital that Rhuaridh wasn't going to give them any chance to prepare, lightwise, soundwise or anything-wise. It was almost as if he was determined to ignore them.

Gerry murmured, 'I can work around him.'

Kristie straightened her spine. If she didn't start to get some decent filming soon she could kiss her career goodbye. But there was a little fire of anger burning down inside her. She didn't let people ignore her. And she'd checked the contract, she knew exactly what Dr Gillespie was getting in return for doing this. He *owed* her three days of filming every month, and if this guy didn't start to deliver, she wouldn't hesitate to remind him.

But Kristie knew, at least for now, she should try and ease him into this filming. Maybe the guy was nervous. Maybe he was shy. Or maybe the guy was just a jerk. Part of her was mad. Did he have any idea how hard she was finding this? Obviously not. But whatever it was that was eating him, she had less than a day and a half to find out.

'So, Dr Gillespie, can you tell me about the first patient we'll be seeing?'

She could see the muscles under his white shirt tense. The ones around the base of his neck were particularly prominent. She nodded to Gerry to keep filming as Rhuaridh muttered a few unintelligible words.

'To the camera, Dr Gillespie,' she said smoothly.

He blinked and turned towards her just as Gerry flicked on their extra light. She almost stepped back. Resentment and annoyance seemed to ooze from every pore. For a second she was sure he was going to say no.

So she moved quickly. 'In fact, let's start with introductions. Face the camera, I'll introduce you, then you can tell the viewers a little about yourself.' She shot him a look, then added in a quiet voice, 'And don't mumble.'

She would never normally do things like this. Usually she would go over all the introductory questions with their subject, check their responses, and make sure everyone was comfortable before they started filming. But the fact was—on this occasion—they just didn't have the time.

Before he had a chance to object she turned to the camera and gave her widest smile. 'Hi, there, folks. It's Kristie Nelson here, and I'm your host for...' She realised her mistake almost instantly, but no one watching would notice it. Did this guy know he was going to be called a Hot Highland Doc for the next year? Maybe better to keep some things quiet, this was already an uphill struggle.

She was smooth. She'd been doing this too long. '*A Year in the Life of...*' She let her voice tail off and held both hands towards Rhuaridh. 'Our doctor. And here he is, this is Rhuaridh Gillespie and he works on the Isle of Arran. Dr Gillespie, can you tell us a little bit about your background and the work that you do?'

Rhuaridh did his best impression of a deer in the headlights. She gave him a little nudge in the ribs and he actually started.

He stared at the camera. Gerry kept it still while he stuck his head out from behind the viewfinder and mouthed, 'Go,' to him.

Rhuaridh gave the tiniest shudder that Kristie was sure only she could see before he started talking. 'Yes, hi, thanks. I'm Rhuaridh Gillespie. I grew up on this island—Arran— before leaving to train in Glasgow as a doctor, then I've worked in a number of other hospitals, and for Doctors Without Borders. I trained as a GP—a general practitioner—like my father, then came back last year to take over the practice when my father...' he paused for a split second before quickly finding a word '...retired.'

She was surprised. He was doing better than expected, even though he still looked as though he didn't want to be there.

'Can you tell the viewers a little about Arran?' she asked.

'It's an island,' he said, as though she'd just asked a ridiculous question.

She kept the smile firmly in place. 'Can you tell the viewers a little about the people here, and the hospital? What was it like growing up here?' The curses shooting across her brain stayed firmly hidden.

He gave a slow nod as if he finally understood that most people watching wouldn't have a single clue about Arran. 'Growing up here was...' his eyes looked up to the left '...fun. Free. Yeah, as a child I had a lot of freedom.

Everyone knows everyone in Arran...' he gave a half-smile '...so there's not much you can get away with. But a normal day was getting on my bike and disappearing into the hillsides with my friends. The lifestyle here is very outdoors.' He gave a small frown. 'Not everyone likes that.'

She wasn't entirely sure what he meant by that but didn't push. 'And the island?' she asked again.

It was almost like his professional face slid back into place. 'The population is around five thousand people, but in the summer months that can quadruple. We have a small cottage hospital with some long-stay beds and a small A and E department. I share the work in the hospital with the other GP on the island.'

'What happens in an emergency?' asked Kristie.

He looked a little uncomfortable. 'If it's a real emergency, then we send the patient off the island by air ambulance. In other circumstances we send people by road ambulance on the ferry and on to the local district general hospital.'

'How long does that take?' She could see a dozen potential stories forming in her head.

Now he was starting to look annoyed. 'The ferry takes around an hour. The transfer from Ardrossan—where the ferry docks—and the local hospital takes around thirty minutes.'

'Wow, that could be dangerous.'

His eyes flashed. 'Not at all. We assess all our patients and make sure they are fit for the transfer before they are sent.'

'What about people needing surgeries or baby emergencies?' She knew there was another word for that but just couldn't think of it.

'Most surgeries are pre-planned and our patients will have made arrangements to go to the mainland. All pregnant women on the island are assessed by both an obstetrician and their midwife. We've had a number of planned home deliveries on the island. Any woman who has a history that would give cause for concern for her, or for her baby, has arrangements made for admission to the mainland hospital to ensure the equipment and staff required are there for her delivery. We haven't had any problems.'

Dull. This place was sounding decidedly dull. All the good stuff—the interesting stuff—got sent to the mainland. But there were a hundred documentary-style shows that covered A and

E departments. How on earth was she going to make this show interesting enough for people to keep watching?

She licked her lips and turned to the computer on top of Rhuaridh's case note trolley. 'So, Dr Gillespie, let's go back. Can you tell us about the first patient we'll be seeing?'

She had to keep this moving. Interesting footage seemed to be slipping through her fingers like grains of sand on the cold beach outside. *Please let this get better.*

There was not a single thing about this that he liked. Her American accent was beginning to grate on him. 'Don't mumble' she'd had the cheek to say to him. He'd never mumbled in his life. At least, he didn't think that he had.

That spotlight had been on him as he'd done the ward round in the cottage hospital. Normally it would have taken half an hour, but her incessant questions had slowed him down more than he'd liked.

She'd kept stopping and talking in a quiet voice to her cameraman and that had irritated him probably a whole lot more than it should have.

He was almost chanting the words in his head. *One more day. One more day.*

One of the nurses from the ward came and found him. 'Rhuaridh, there's been a message left to remind you about your home visit.'

'Darn it.' John Henderson. He still hadn't managed to drop in on him. He shook his head and grabbed his jacket and case.

'What? Where are you going?' Kristie wrinkled her nose. 'What's a home visit anyway?'

He stared at the woman standing under his nose who was almost blocking his way to the exit. He felt guilty. He'd meant to visit John before he came here, but this filming thing had distracted him in a way he hadn't been before.

He snapped, 'It's when you visit someone—at home.' He couldn't help the way he said the words. What on earth else could a home visit be?

Kristie only looked insulted for a few seconds. 'You actually do that here?'

Of course. She was from the US. It was a totally different healthcare system. They generally saw a specialist for everything. Doctors like him—general practitioners who occasionally visited sick patients at home—were unheard of.

'Of course.' He elbowed past her and moved out to his car.

'Let's go,' he heard her squeak to her colleague, and within a few seconds he heard their feet thudding behind him.

He spun around and held up his hand. 'You can't come.'

She tilted her chin upwards obstinately. 'We can.' She turned her notes towards him. 'John Henderson, he's on the list of patients that granted permission for us to film.'

Of course. Pam had already put a system in place to keep track of all this.

He couldn't really say no—no matter how much he wanted to. He shook his head, resigned to his fate.

'Okay, get in the car but we need to go now.'

They piled into the back of his car and he set off towards the farm where John Henderson lived.

It was almost like she didn't know when to stop talking. Kristie started immediately. 'So, can you brief us on this patient before we get there?'

Rhuaridh gritted his teeth. It was late, he was tired. He didn't want to 'brief' them on John Henderson, the elderly farmer with the biggest range of health problems in the world. He was trying to work out how he hadn't managed to fit John in before the visit to the hospital. He should have. Normally, he would have. But today he'd been—distracted.

And Rhuaridh Gillespie had never been distracted before. Not even when he'd been a junior doctor juggling a hundred tasks.

He didn't speak. He could hear her breathing just behind his ear, leaning forward expectantly and waiting for some kind of answer. Eventually he heard a little sigh of frustration and she must have sat back as the waft of orange blossom scent he'd picked up from her earlier disappeared.

The road to the farm was like every road to a farm on Arran. Winding, dark, with numerous potholes and part way up a hill. This was why he needed the four-by-four.

He pulled up outside the farmhouse and frowned. There was one light inside, in what he knew was the main room. John usually had the place lit up like the Blackpool Illuminations. They liked to joke about it.

He jumped out, not waiting for his entourage to follow, knocking loudly at the front door and only waiting a few seconds before pushing it open.

'John, it's Rhuaridh. Everything okay?'

There was a whimper at his feet and his heart sank as he turned. Mac, John's old sheepdog, usually rushed to meet anyone who appeared at the farm, barking loudly, but now he was whimpering in the hall.

He bent down, rubbed the black and white dog's head. 'What's up, Mac?'

Even as he said the words he had a horrible feeling that he knew what the answer would be.

He was familiar with the old farmhouse, having visited here numerous times in the last few months. Mac stayed at his heels as he walked through to the main room. It was shambolic. Had been for the last few years, ever since John's wife had died and he'd refused any kind of help.

The sofa was old and worn, the rug a little threadbare. A few pictures hung on the walls.

But his eyes fixed on the sight he didn't want to see.

'John!' He rushed across the room, already knowing it would make no difference as he knelt on the floor beside the crumpled body of the old man. Mac lay down right next to John, still whimpering as he put his head on John's back.

John's colour was completely dusky. His lips blue. 'Here, boy,' said Rhuaridh gently as he pushed Mac's head away and turned John over onto his back.

His body was still warm, probably thanks to the flickering fire. But there were absolutely no signs of life. No breathing. No heartbeat. He did all the checks he needed to, but it was clear to him that John had died a few hours before.

It didn't matter that this had been on the cards for a number of months. With his cardiac and respiratory disease John had been living on borrowed time for a while. But the fact was Rhuaridh had loved this old crotchety guy, with his gnarled hands through years of hard work and the well-weathered, lined face.

He looked peaceful now. His face more un-lined than Rhuaridh had ever seen it before.

Something inside Rhuaridh ached. John had died alone. Something he'd always been afraid of. If Rhuaridh had got here earlier—if he hadn't taken so long over the hospital ward round—he might have made it in time to hold his hand for his last few breaths.

He lifted John's coldish hand and clasped it between both of his. 'I'm sorry,' he whispered before he moved and closed John's eyelids with one finger. He couldn't help the tear he had to brush away. Mac moved back and put his head on John's chest. He hadn't thought it possible for a dog to look quite as sad as Mac did now.

He pulled his phone from his back pocket and made the obligatory phone call. 'Donald, yes, it's Rhuaridh Gillespie. I've just found John Henderson. Yes, I think he's been dead for a couple of hours. You will? Thank you. I'll wait until you get here.'

He sighed and pushed his phone into his pocket then started at the sound behind him.

Gerry had his camera on his shoulder and Kristie was wide-eyed. She looked almost shocked. A wave of anger swept over him. 'Put that away. It's hardly appropriate.'

Gerry pulled the camera to one side. Kristie

seemed frozen to the spot. She lifted one shaking hand towards the body on the floor. 'Is…is that it? There's…nothing you can do?' It was the first time her voice hadn't been assured and full of confidence.

'Of course there's nothing I can do,' he snapped. 'John's been dead for the last few hours.'

He didn't add the thoughts that were currently streaming through his brain. *If she hadn't delayed him at the hospital, maybe he could have been here earlier. If she hadn't distracted him at the doctor's surgery, maybe he would have made John's visit before he went to the hospital.*

He knew this was all irrational. But that didn't make it go away.

Gerry's voice broke through his thoughts. 'Do you have to wait for the police?'

Rhuaridh nodded. 'They'll be here in a few minutes, and the undertaker will probably arrive at the same time.'

He turned his attention back to John and knelt down beside him again, resting his hand on John's chest. He felt odd about all of this. They'd stopped filming but it still felt like they were...intruding. And it was he who had brought them here.

Gerry seemed to have a knack of fading into the shadows, but Kristie? She stood out like a sore thumb. Or something else entirely. He'd been around plenty of beautiful, confident women in his life. What was so different about this one? She felt like a permanent itch that had got under his skin. Probably not the nicest description in the world but certainly the most accurate.

She stood to the side with her eyes fixed on the floor at first as his police colleague arrived then Craig, the undertaker. The unfortunate part of being a GP was that for he, and his two colleagues, this was semi-familiar territory.

When at last things were sorted and John's body was ready to be loaded into the undertaker's car, it was almost like the others knew and stepped back for a few seconds.

'What about Mac?' asked Donald, the police officer.

'Right.' For a few seconds Rhuaridh looked around. There was no one to take care of Mac, and they probably all knew that.

He looked over at the dog lying dolefully on

the rug, his head on his paws. It didn't matter how impractical. How ridiculous. 'Give me a second.' He moved back over to John's body and slid his hand in to find the keys for the house in John's trouser pocket. Someone would need to lock up.

He stepped back to allow them to take John's body out to the hearse, then moved through to the kitchen and grabbed a bag, stuffing into it the dog's bowl and a few tins of dog food from the cupboard.

Kristie and Gerry were still hanging around in the hallway, Gerry still with the camera resting carelessly on his shoulder.

'You good?' Donald asked as Rhuaridh appeared back out of the kitchen.

He nodded and walked through to the main room. It was almost as if Mac knew because he jumped up and walked over, tail giving a few wags as he wound his body around Rhuaridh's legs.

'Come on then, old guy,' Rhuaridh said as he patted Mac's head. 'Looks like it's you and me.' He bent down and paused for a few seconds, his head next to Mac's. Mac had lived on a farm his whole life. How would he like living in a cottage by the beach? A wave of sympathy and affection flooded through him as he looked at Mac's big brown eyes. Of course he had to take this guy home.

It only took a few moments to put out the fire, flick the lights switches and lock the main door. Mac jumped into the back seat next to Gerry, who seemed quite happy to pat Mac on the drive back.

He dropped them at their rental and sped off into the dark as quickly as he could. His first day of filming couldn't have been worse. 'Please don't let them all be like this,' he murmured to Mac.

Kristie watched the car speed away. Her feet seemed frozen and she didn't even care about the brisk wind blowing around her. After a few seconds, Gerry slung his arm around her shoulders. She'd just seen her second dead body. And she couldn't work out how she felt about that—except numb. It was evoking memories that she just didn't want to recall. The little old man's house had been so…real. A few hours earlier he'd been there, and then he was just…gone.

This was exactly why she hadn't wanted to

do this job. It was touching at places she kept firmly hidden, pulling at strings in her memory that she preferred not to remember. She shivered, and it wasn't from the cold.

Gerry looked at the red lights on the now far-off car. 'Funny kind of guy, isn't he?'

Anger surged inside her. 'He's got a contract. They're getting paid well for this.'

Gerry looked at her in amusement and shook his head, taking his hand off her shoulder and instead tapping the camera in his other hand.

'You haven't realised, have you?'

She shook her head. She had no idea what he was talking about.

Gerry smiled. 'That stiff-faced, crotchety doc guise that he's pulling. This? This tears it all apart.' He gave another nod of his head. 'Kristie Nelson, in here, we have TV gold.'

CHAPTER TWO

June

THE FERRY WAS much busier this time. It seemed that hordes of schoolchildren seemed to be going on some kind of trip.

An older woman sat next to her, sipping a cup of tea. This time Kristie had been prepared for the ferry crossing, and her anti-sickness tablets seemed to be doing the trick. The older woman smiled. 'There's an outdoor centre. They're all going there to stay for a week. I guarantee tonight not one of them will sleep. But after their first day on Arran tomorrow, they'll all be sleeping by nine o'clock.'

Kristie nodded half-heartedly. She wasn't really paying attention. Last night she'd watched the edited first show about the Hot Highland Doc.

For want of a better word—it had been dynamite.

The editing had helped, showing the crabbit doctor—a definitely unwilling participant in the show—turning to a melting puddle of emotion at the death of his elderly patient. The final shot that Gerry had sneaked of him connecting with Mac the dog and saying the words, 'Looks like it's just you and me,' would melt the proverbial hearts of the nation when it was shown in a few weeks.

Louie couldn't contain his excitement. 'Play on the fact he doesn't like you.'

Kristie had been a bit stung. 'What do you mean, he doesn't like me?' She hadn't realised it was quite so obvious to anyone but her.

'The audience will love it. You against him. The sparks are tremendous.'

Kristie bit her bottom lip as the announcement came for them all to head to their cars. Last time she'd been desperate to capture anything on camera.

This time around she felt the pressure. The producers didn't just like it, they *loved* it. Apparently the limited footage they'd captured had been the most entertaining—in a heart-wrenching kind of way—of any of the other *Year in the Life of* shows. They hadn't, of course, shown

John Henderson. Gerry had filmed Rhuaridh from the back, leaning over the body, without revealing anything about the identity of the patient.

He'd also filmed 'around' Rhuaridh, capturing the essence of the home and the situation, with a particular focus on Mac, and how the professionals had dealt with everything, without sticking the camera in their faces. Kristie was a tiny bit nervous what people would think about it when it finally aired—but she knew it had squeezed at even her heart.

She climbed into the car with Gerry and gave him a nod, handing him a schedule. 'I've had time to be in touch a bit more. We're spending some time in the A and E department in the cottage hospital and filming one of the regular surgeries this time.'

He gave a nod. 'Here's hoping we get something good.' He raised one eyebrow. 'No pressure, of course.'

She shot him a glare. He was being sarcastic, of course.

'Where are we staying?'

Gerry wrinkled his nose. 'We've got a bed and breakfast this time—just down the road from the surgery.' His eyes twinkled. 'Guess we won't need to live on cereal for three days this time.'

She laughed. Neither she nor Gerry was blessed with cooking skills. 'I've decided. We're eating out every night and putting it on expenses.'

He nodded in agreement, 'Oh, I can live with that.'

They settled into the bed and breakfast quickly and made their way to the surgery for their scheduled filming. It was obvious news had spread since the last time they'd been there as a number of the patients sitting in the waiting room started talking to them as soon as they appeared.

'Are you the TV people?'

'Do you want to film me?'

'When will I be on TV?'

'Oh, you're here.' Her head shot up. It was hardly the most welcoming statement. Rhuaridh was standing in the doorway of his surgery dressed in a white shirt and navy trousers. It looked like he'd caught the sun in the last few days as his skin was more tanned than before.

Her first instinct was to hear a wolf whistle in her head. If her friend Alice had been here she was sure she would have actually done it in real life. One thing was for sure—Rhuaridh Gillespie was like a good old-fashioned prom king standing right in front of her.

But then her mouth dried. For a few seconds all she could remember was how she'd felt last time she'd been around him and he'd been dealing with Mr Henderson's dead body. She tried so hard not to let the others notice her reaction. Of course, Gerry had picked up on it. But he hadn't asked any questions.

The surgery filming went fine. For the first few patients it was obvious Rhuaridh wasn't a natural in front of the camera. Eventually, though, he seemed to forget they were there. But filming blood-pressure checks, medicine reviews, chest infections and leg ulcers didn't exactly make scintillating viewing. Kristie could feel a small wave of panic start to build inside.

By the time the day had come to an end she wasn't sure they had enough for even ten minutes of not very interesting film. She was just about to clarify their arrangements for the next day when Rhuaridh's pager sounded.

He looked just as surprised as she did. He

hadn't been wearing one the last time she'd been there. A deep frown creased his forehead. It took him a few seconds to look up and speak once he'd checked the message. He gave his head a little shake. 'I thought it was for the local lifeboat…but it's not…it's Magda.'

He looked around his room blankly for a few seconds. Was this a sign of panic? She would never have suspected it from Rhuaridh Gillespie—and who on earth was Magda? A wife? A girlfriend? He hadn't mentioned either last time and she couldn't help but be a tiny bit disappointed. Within another few seconds the look was gone. He strode quickly across the waiting room, grabbing his bag. Kristie stayed on his heels, waving Gerry to follow. If this was something good, she wanted to make sure they didn't miss it.

He shot her a glance as she opened the back door of his car to climb inside. She saw the words form on his lips—the words of dismissal—but she completely ignored him, turning to shout to Gerry instead, 'Let's go!'

It seemed for Rhuaridh it wasn't worth the time involved in fighting. Gerry had barely slammed the door before he took off at speed onto the main road in Lamlash. As they started to drive, his phone started ringing. He answered with a press on his steering wheel. 'Miriam, are you with her?'

'Of course. How far away are you?'

'Less than two minutes.'

'Good.' The phone went dead.

Kristie was immediately intrigued. 'Who are you visiting?'

Rhuaridh's jaw was clenched. 'My colleague, Magda. She's planned for a home delivery but things are looking complicated.'

Gerry shot her a look. There was a gleam in his eye. This would be more interesting filming than what they'd already got.

Kristie tried her best to phrase the question carefully. She obviously wanted the footage—but didn't want to get in the way if something could go wrong. Even she had a line that wouldn't be crossed.

'We didn't get to meet your colleague,' she started.

Rhuaridh cut her off. 'You should have—she was the one who signed up for the show. Her pregnancy was an unexpected but very happy event.'

Gerry gave her a thumbs-up in the back of the car. If Magda had initially signed for the show, she might not object to being filmed. There was something in the way Rhuaridh said the words. He had an obvious affection for his colleague.

They pulled up outside a large white house at the end of a long driveway. The front door was open and Kristie gestured to Gerry to get his camera on his shoulder ready to film.

They jumped out of the car and she hesitated as she heard the voices inside.

'Don't panic, Magda, let's get you out right now and I'll attach a CTG to monitor the baby. Now take a deep breath and try not to worry.'

She glanced at Gerry. Yip. He was already filming, capturing the sound inside.

Rhuaridh strode straight inside. Then stopped dead, meaning Kristie walked into the back of him.

'Oh, sorry.'

The main room of the house appeared to have undergone a complete transformation for the delivery of this baby. Right in the centre of the room was a large birthing pool. Soothing music was playing in the background, the blinds were closed and there were a few lit candles.

A heavily pregnant woman with blonde hair and a black loose wet kaftan was being helped from the pool by a worried-looking man and an older woman.

The woman looked up. 'Give me a hand, Rhuaridh.'

He stepped over quickly, taking the woman's place as she dropped to her knees and pulled a small monitor from a black case.

They eased Magda down onto the nearby sofa. Obviously no one was worried about getting it entirely wet.

'Tell me what's happening,' said Rhuaridh.

Kristie was tempted to clear her throat and remind them all that two perfect strangers were in the room, but the woman she thought was Magda looked up and waved her hand in a throwaway manner. 'Carry on,' she said as she grimaced.

'Another one?' asked the woman quickly.

Magda nodded and gripped tightly onto the man Kristie suspected was her husband.

Rhuaridh finally seemed to remember they were there. He pointed at his friends. 'Magda, David, Miriam, this is Kristie and Gerry from the TV show.'

Since Magda had already waved her hand in permission it seemed like he didn't feel the need to say anything else.

Kristie could see the way that David was looking at Rhuaridh. It was odd. She was brand new to these people but could already see a world of emotion without hearing any words. David was holding back panic, Magda had an edge of fear about her, and Miriam—who must be the midwife—had her professional face in place, while worry seemed etched on the lines on her forehead.

Rhuaridh knelt by the sofa and held Magda's hand. 'I thought you had this planned to pre-cision.'

She patted her stomach, keeping her eyes firmly fixed on Miriam's actions as she attached the monitor. 'It seems Baby Price has his or her own plans.'

Miriam spoke in a low voice as she made the final adjustments. 'Spontaneous rupture of membrane a few hours ago. Labour has been progressing well with no concerns. Magda's around eight centimetres dilated, but she feels baby has stopped moving in the last ten minutes.'

'It's a boy,' said Rhuaridh. 'He's having a little sleep before the big event.' The hoarseness in his voice gripped Kristie around the chest. He was worried. He was worried about his friend's baby.

Magda tutted. 'We don't know it's a boy. We want a surprise.'

She was scared to make eye contact with Gerry. This was beginning to feel like a bad idea. An old man tragedy she'd almost been able to bear. Anything with a baby? No way.

Miriam flicked the switch and the monitor flickered to life. After a few seconds a noise filled the room. Kristie almost let out a cheer. Even she could recognise the sound of a heartbeat.

But the rest of the room didn't seem quite so joyous. Magda clenched her teeth as she was obviously gripped with a new contraction.

All other eyes in the room seemed fixed on the monitor. Kristie leaned forward, trying to see the number on the screen. Ninety, wasn't that good?

'What's happening?' asked Magda.

There was sense in the room of collective

breath-holding. The numbers on the screen and the corresponding beat noises crept upwards.

Rhuaridh and Miriam whispered almost in unison. 'Cord prolapse.'

This was all way above Kristie's head.

Magda let out a small squeak of desperation. 'No.' As a doctor it seemed she knew exactly what that could mean even if Kristie didn't.

Rhuaridh pulled out his phone and dialled. 'Air ambulance. Obstetric emergency.' His voice was low and calm. He moved over to the corner of the room where Kristie couldn't hear him any more. By the time he'd finished, David had walked towards him.

'Tell me what's happening.'

Rhuaridh nodded. 'The cord is coming down the birth canal before, or adjacent to, the baby. It means that every time Magda has a contraction, there's a risk the cord can be compressed and affect the blood flow to your baby.'

'Our baby could die?' David's words were little more than a squeak.

Rhuaridh shook his head, but Kristie could see the tense muscles at the bottom of his neck. The tiny hairs prickled on her skin. She was useless here—no help whatsoever. What did she know about medical emergencies?

She walked over to the window and looked outside, putting her hands on her hips and taking a few breaths.

The midwife's voice cut across momentary panic. 'Magda, we're going to change your position. Kristie!' The voice was sharp—one you wouldn't hesitate to follow. 'Run upstairs to the bedroom and grab me all the pillows on the bed.'

Rhuaridh finished his call and moved over to help move Magda onto her side. Kristie did exactly what she'd been told and dashed up the stairs in the house, turning one way then the other until she found the room with the large double bed and grabbed every pillow on it. She paused for the briefest of seconds as her eyes focused on the little white Moses basket at the side of the bed. The basket that had been placed there with the hope and expectation of a beautiful baby.

She held back the sob in her throat as she ran back down the stairs and thrust the pillows towards Rhuaridh. He and Miriam moved in unison. Rhuaridh spoke in a low voice as he helped adjust Magda's position with some pillows under her left flank and her right knee and thigh pulled up towards her chest. 'The position is supposed to alleviate pressure on the umbilical cord.' His words were quiet and Kristie wasn't sure if he was explaining to her or to David.

Magda's hands were trembling slightly. She was scared and Kristie's heart went out to her. How must this feel? All of a sudden this felt like a real intrusion instead of a filming opportunity. How dared they be there right now?

Rhuaridh's gaze connected with hers. She wasn't quite sure what she was reading there. His voice seemed a little steely. 'Gerry, the air ambulance will land in the field next to the house—you might want to get that.' Gerry nodded and was gone in the blink of an eye.

She was still looking at those bright blue eyes, trying to control the overwhelming sensation of being utterly useless in a situation completely out of her area of expertise. Right now all she could do was send up a prayer that both Magda and this baby would be fine. It was amazing how quickly a set of circumstances could envelop you. Was this what every day was like for a doctor?

All of a sudden she had a new understanding of her grumpy doctor. This was a situation he could end up in any day, and today it involved a friend. She could almost sense the history in the room between them all. The long-standing friendship, along with the expectations. If something happened to Magda or this baby, things would never be the same again.

The monitor for the baby kept pinging. At least that was reassuring. Miriam and Rhuaridh had a conversation about whether another examination should be carried out. Both agreed not, though Kristie averted her gaze while Miriam did a quick visual check to reassure that no cord was protruding.

Rhuaridh moved over next to her and she caught a whiff of his woody aftershave. 'What's gone wrong?' Kristie whispered. Magda was holding her husband's hand, her eyes fixed on the monitor that showed the baby's heartbeat.

Rhuaridh spoke in a low, quiet voice. 'Magda wasn't at high risk for anything. She'd planned for this home birth within an inch of her life. Cord prolapse is unusual, and Magda has no apparent risk factors. But, right now, every time she has a contraction, the baby's heartbeat goes down, meaning the cord is being compressed.'

'Can't you do anything?'

He shook his head. 'The cord isn't obviously protruding, so we just need to get Magda to hospital as soon as possible. This baby needs to be delivered and Magda will need to have a Caesarean section.' He ran his hand through his hair, the frustration on his face evident. 'We just don't have the facilities here for that—or the expertise.'

'How long does the air ambulance take to get here?'

'Usually not long,' he said, then looked upwards as a thud-thud-thud noise could be heard in the distance.

Kristie's heart started thudding in her chest. Maybe everything was actually going to be okay?

Magda let out a groan, and Kristie held her breath as she watched Rhuaridh and Miriam move to support her as she was hit by another contraction. All eyes were on the monitor, and although the heart rate went down, it didn't go down quite as much as it had before.

Rhuaridh glanced towards the door a few times. Kristie could see him weighing up whether to ask David to go and meet the crew or whether to go himself.

After a few seconds he squeezed Magda's hand. 'Give me a minute.' Then he jogged out the main door and across towards the field. Kristie couldn't help but follow him. Gerry had positioned himself outside to capture the landing and the crew emerging from the helicopter.

They didn't waste any time. Within a few minutes Rhuaridh and Miriam had helped keep Magda into the correct position as they assisted her onto the trolley. The CTG monitor was swapped over for another and then Magda and David disappeared inside the helicopter before it lifted off into the air.

They all stood watching the helicopter disappear into the distance, Gerry with his camera firmly on his shoulder.

Once the helicopter finally vanished from view there were a few moments of awkward silence. They all turned and looked at the open door of the house. Miriam was first to move, walking back into the house, putting her hands on her hips and taking a deep breath.

The space felt huge and empty without Magda. The birthing pool lay with only its rippling water, monitors, blood-pressure cuff, the midwife's case and Rhuaridh's, all alongside the normal family furnishings. Pictures of David and Magda on their wedding day. The sofa with the now squelchy cushions. A multitude of towels.

'I guess we'd better clean up,' said Kristie.

She wasn't quite sure where that had come from. Cleaning up was definitely not her forte.

She bent down and lifted one of the sofa cushions, wondering if she should take it to the kitchen to try and clean it off and dry it out.

Miriam had started picking up all the midwifery equipment.

Rhuaridh appeared in front of her and grabbed the cushion. 'Leave it. We'll get it. You should just go.'

She blinked. Wondered what on earth she'd just done wrong. She'd just witnessed a scene that had almost made her blood run cold. Had she ever been as scared as this?

Yes. Probably. But that part of her brain was compartmentalised and knowingly put away. It was better that way. It felt safer that way. The only time she let little parts of it emerge was when she volunteered three nights a month on the helpline. It was the only time she let down her guard. Virtually no one knew about that part of her life. Louie did. He'd been there for her when she'd got the original phone call telling her to come to the hospital. Gerry had been there too.

Louie had held her hand in the waiting room. He'd put an arm around her when she'd been given the news, and he'd stood at the door as she'd had to go and identify her sister's body.

Her beautiful, gorgeous, fun-loving sister. She almost hadn't recognised her on the table. Her skin had been pale with an ugly purple mark on her neck. When she'd touched her sister's hand it had been cold and stiff. The scars on her sister's wrists and inside her elbows had taken her breath away.

Everything had been new to her. She'd had no idea about the self-harm. She'd had no idea her sister had been depressed. Jess had hidden all of this from her—to all intents from everyone. It had only been a long time afterwards when she'd been left to empty her sister's apartment and go through her things that she'd discovered a frequently phoned number that was unfamiliar. The thing that had pricked her attention most had been the number of times that Jess had phoned—and yet had disconnected the calls in under a minute. That's when she'd discovered the helpline.

It was situated in their city and manned by counsellors and trained mental health professionals, staffed twenty-four hours a day. One visit to the centre had made her realise she had to try and help too. She'd undergone her training, and now manned the phone lines three nights a month. The small hours of the morning were sometimes the busiest in the call centre. She'd learned when to talk, and when not to. She'd learned that sometimes people just wanted to know that someone had heard them cry. Had *heard* them at all.

It always took her back to the fact that she wished Jess had stayed on the line a little longer—just once. It might have made the difference. It might have let her know she was safe to confide how she was feeling and didn't have to hide it.

Occasionally she would get a flashback to part of that first night. Hospitals were a place she'd generally avoided ever since, associating the sights and sounds with the memories of that night. It was part of the reason she'd been reluctant about this gig.

But now she was realising it was something more. Last month, with John Henderson's body, and this time, when she'd glanced at the cot upstairs—patiently waiting for its baby—she'd felt a sweep of something else. Pure and utter dread. The kind that made her heart beat faster and her breathing kind of funny.

Her heart had sunk as the helicopter had disappeared into the distance, not knowing what the outcome would be for Magda and the baby. She didn't care about the show right now. She didn't care about anything.

And all that she could see was this great hulking man standing in front of her with the strangest expression on his face. His hands brushed against hers as he closed them around the cushion, gripping it.

He gave a tug towards himself. 'I think it would be best if you go now.'

She couldn't understand. 'But the room...' She let go of the cushion and held out her hands, looking over at the birthing pool and wondering how on earth it would be emptied and taken down. 'You'll need help to clean up.'

She wanted distraction. She wanted something else to think about. Anything to keep her mind busy until there was news about mother and baby.

'I'm sure Magda and David would prefer that their house be fixed up by friends.' He emphasised the word so strongly that she took a step backwards and stumbled, putting a steadying hand on the window frame behind her.

It was then she saw it. The flash across his face. He needed distraction just as much as she did. Probably more. He must be worried sick. Of course he was.

She'd only just met this pregnant woman. He'd known her for—how long? She wouldn't even like to guess. She knew they'd been workmates in the practice but she hadn't really had a chance to hear much more.

'I want you to go now,' he said as he turned away. 'We'll let you know how things are.'

It was a dismissal. Blunt. She wanted to grab him by the arm and yank him around, ask him who he thought he was talking to. In another life she might have.

But if she fell out with Dr Gillespie the whole show could be up in the air. So instead she pressed her lips together and looked around for her bag, grabbing it and throwing it over her shoulder, walking out the room and leaving the disarray behind her.

Gerry was standing at the door. She didn't care if the camera was on or not. 'I hate him,' she hissed in a low voice as she walked past.

Rhuaridh knew he'd just been unreasonable. He knew that Magda had agreed to the TV crew filming. But none of them had expected the outcome that had just happened.

His heart felt twisted in a hard, angry knot. Every possible scenario was running through his head right now—and not all of them were good.

He wasn't an obstetrician. The limited experience he'd had had been gained when he'd been a junior doctor. He knew the basics. He knew the basics of a lot of things. But island communities were different from most. The water cut them off from the mainland. There was no quick road to a hospital with a whole variety of specialists and equipment at his disposal.

In the last few months there had been a mountain climber with a severe head injury, a few elderly residents with hip fractures, a diver with decompression sickness, and now an obstetric emergency. All situations where he'd felt helpless—useless even. He hated that his patients needed to wait for either a ferry crossing or an air ambulance to take them where they could get the help required. He hated that he had to stand and look into their eyes, knowing that on occasion that help might actually be too late. And today, when it had been his friend and colleague, he had felt as though he was being gripped around the chest by a vice.

He'd snapped needlessly at Kristie. He knew that. But he just couldn't think beyond what would happen next for Magda, David and the baby. And until he knew that, he didn't know what came next.

Guilt swamped him. 'Kristie, wait,' he shouted as he walked out after her.

She spun around towards him. The expression in her eyes told him everything he needed to know. She was every bit as panicked and worried as he was. She was also mad. And no wonder. He knew better than to act like this.

He walked over and put a hand on her shoulder. 'I'm sorry,' he said quickly. 'I'm just worried.' He glanced up at the sky. The helicopter was well out of sight. He prayed things would go well. 'I didn't mean to snap. And thank you for your help in there. I just feel so…' He struggled to say the word out loud, not really wanting to admit it.

'Helpless?' Kristie added without hesitation. He could see her eyes searching his face. Wondering if he would agree.

He closed his eyes for a second and nodded as the rush of adrenalin seemed to leave his body all at once. 'Helpless,' he agreed with a sigh. 'I won't be able to think about another thing until I know they're both okay.'

'Neither will I,' she said quickly. Should he really be surprised? It was the first real time since she'd got here that he'd taken the time to really look at her, *really* see something other than the bolshie American TV presenter. There was something there. Something he couldn't quite put his finger on.

Her hand reached across her chest and covered the hand he had on her shoulder. He felt a jolt. It must be the warmth of her palm against his cold skin. She licked her bare lips. All her makeup had disappeared in the last few hours. She didn't need it. Something sparked in his brain. Had he really just thought that?

She squeezed his hand and spoke quietly as she held his gaze. 'Let's just do the only thing we can. Pray.'

His stomach gave a gentle flip as he nodded in agreement and looked back up at the sky. He pushed everything else away. Magda and the baby were all he could concentrate on right now. Anything else could wait.

CHAPTER THREE

July

PEOPLE WERE LOOKING at him a bit strangely, and he couldn't quite work out why. And it wasn't just the people he knew. Summer holidays had well and truly started and, as normal, the island's population had grown, bringing a stream of holidaymakers with minor complaints and medical issues to the island's GP surgery. This meant that he now had a whole host of strangers giving him strange sideways glances that turned into odd smiles.

It took one older lady with a chest infection to reveal the source.

'You're the handsome doc I saw on TV,' she said.

'What?' He was sounding the woman's chest at that point, paying attention to the auscultations of her lungs instead of to her voice.

She gave a loud tut then giggled. 'You really don't like that poor girl, do you?'

He pulled the stethoscope from his ears. 'Excuse me?'

'The pretty one. With the blonde hair. She looked shell-shocked by that death.' The woman leaned over and patted his hand. 'I'm sorry about your friend. How's Mac?'

For a few moments, Rhuaridh was stunned. Then the penny dropped like a cannonball on his head.

'You've seen the TV show?' He hadn't really paid attention to when it would air.

She grinned. 'Yes. It was wonderful. Best episode of that series yet.' She gave him a sideways glance and raised her eyebrows. 'And, yep, it's probably fair that they call you hot. But you really need to behave a bit better.'

He wasn't really paying attention to all her words. 'What do you mean—the death?'

She frowned at him, as though he were a little dense. 'Your friend. The farmer.'

'They showed that?' He felt a surge of anger. How dared they?

The old woman shook her head. 'Well, we didn't really see anything much at all. Just a pair of feet. Nothing else. It was more about…' she held her hands up to her crackly chest '…the feelings, the emotions. The love in the room.' She gave a wicked little shrug. 'And the tension. Like I said, you need to be nicer to that girl. She's very pretty, you know. She looked as though she could have done with a hug.'

Rhuaridh sat back in his chair. He was stunned. He'd kind of thought the TV show would only be shown in other countries—not this one. He hadn't expected people he met to have seen it. And he wasn't happy they'd shown the events at John Henderson's house.

The old woman sat back and folded her hands in her lap. 'Mind you, you brought a tear to my eye when you took Mac home with you. How is he, anyway? You didn't answer.'

It was almost like he was being told off. It seemed that parts of his life were now open to public view and scrutiny. Part of him wanted to see the episode—to check it didn't betray John Henderson's memory. But part of him dreaded to see himself on screen. It seemed like he might not have done himself any favours. His insides cringed. 'Mac's good,' he said on autopilot as his brain continued to whirl. 'He's settled in well.'

The old woman gave another tut and looked at him as though he didn't really know what he was doing. 'Well, are you going to write me a prescription or not? Erythromycin, please. It always works best.'

Rhuaridh picked up his prescription pad and pen. This was going to be a long, long day.

The boat was packed to the brim. There was literally not a single seat to be had, and it was lucky someone at the production company had pre-booked their car space and their rental. 'What is it?' said Gerry. 'Has the whole of mainland Scotland decided to visit the island at once?'

'Feels like it,' muttered Kristie as she was jostled by a crowd of holidaymakers. At least the sun was high in the sky and she'd remembered to take her sea sickness tablets.

She leaned on the rail as the ferry started to dock. 'The reception's been good hasn't it?'

Gerry nodded. 'I've not seen this much excitement in a while. And once they've seen the second episode? I think people will go crazy.'

Kristie blew out a long breath. The next episode was due to air in a few weeks. It was ironic really. The first episode had been all about death, and now the second was all about life. They'd improvised. Once they'd left the island, instead of heading straight back to Glasgow airport, they'd driven to the local maternity unit where they'd got Magda's permission to capture a scene with a beautiful healthy baby girl and two relieved, smiling parents. Even Kristie couldn't hide the tears at that point. But it had captured the story perfectly, and would give the viewers the happy ending they would all crave.

'What about me?' she asked Gerry. 'And what about him, what if he sees me saying I hate him?' Her stomach twisted uncomfortably. The producer had insisted on keeping all those elements in, saying the dynamics between her and Rhuaridh Gillespie were TV gold.

Gerry waved his hand as the gangplank was lowered and people started filing off the boat. 'I doubt he's seen it. And if he has? Too bad.'

They made their way down to the car. The car storage area was hot and claustrophobic. Gerry shrugged off his jacket and tugged at his shirt. 'You okay?' she asked.

He nodded. 'Just get me out into the fresh air.'

The plans were a little different this time. They'd agreed to focus more on Rhuaridh's role at the hospital rather than his role at the GP surgery. It seemed harsh, but if they hadn't had the drama with the delivery for the last episode things might have been a little dry.

But for the first day they were going to do some background filming around the hospital. Kristie wasn't sure how that would work out. Or how interesting it would be. At least this time she felt a little prepared and didn't dread it quite so much.

But she shouldn't have worried. The seventeen patients in the cottage hospital were delighted to see her and participate in the filming. She met an army war veteran who had dozens of naughty stories that had her wiping tears from her eyes. She met a young girl who was in the midst of cancer treatment who'd come down with an infection and was bribing the hospital kitchen staff to make her chocolate pancakes. She interviewed the hospital porter, who was eighty and refused to retire. She met a biker who'd come off his bike and fractured his femur. But he'd timed it just as a visiting orthopaedic consultant was doing his monthly clinic on Arran, so had had his surgery performed in the equipped theatre a few hours later.

All this filming without having to deal with Dr Grumpy—as Kristie had nicknamed him.

They'd arranged filming for a little later the next day as they'd been warned the local A and E could be quieter in the mornings. As they pulled up in the hospital car park they could already spot Rhuaridh's car—along with a whole host of others. 'I take it Friday afternoon is a busy time,' said Gerry as they got out of the car.

Kristie shrugged. 'We're trying to get away from the mundane. He's on call all weekend, so maybe we'll get something unusual.'

As they walked inside Gerry almost tripped. The waiting room was almost as busy as yesterday's ferry. He smiled. 'We might be lucky.'

Kristie looked around. 'Let's interview a few of the people waiting,' she said. The waiting room was full of a range of people. There looked like a whole host of bumps and breaks. A few kids had large eggs on their foreheads, others were holding arms a little awkwardly.

Legs were on chairs, and some people were sleeping.

It didn't take long for Rhuaridh to spot them in the waiting room. His perpetual frown creased his forehead, then it was almost like he realised that had happened and he pushed his shoulders back and forced a smile on to his face. 'Kristie, Gerry, come through.'

The normally relatively quiet A and E department was buzzing inside. Names were written on a whiteboard, with times next to them. Three nurses and one advanced nurse practitioner were dealing with patients in the various cubicles.

The charge nurse, June, gave Kristie and Gerry a rundown of what was happening. She motioned to a set of rooms. 'Welcome to the conveyor belt.'

'What do you mean?'

June smiled. 'I mean that slips, fractures and falls are our biggest issue today. Everyone in the waiting room has already been assessed. We generally deal with the kids first, unless something is life threatening, then, if need be, an adult can jump the queue. But most of the people outside are waiting for X-rays, and quite a large proportion of them will go on to need a cast.' She pointed to a room that was deemed the 'plaster room' where one nurse, dressed in an apron, was applying a lightweight coloured fibreglass cast to a kid's wrist. There was another child with a similar injury already waiting outside to go in next.

Another nurse nodded on the way past. 'And I have all the head injuries. So far, nothing serious. But I have four kids and two adults to do neuro obs on for the next few hours.'

Rhuaridh walked up and touched Kristie's arm. 'Do you want to come and film a kid's assessment? He's probably got a broken wrist too, but you could capture the story from start to finish—probably in under an hour.'

Kristie couldn't hide her surprise at his consideration. She exchanged glances with Gerry. 'Well, yeah, that would be great, thanks.'

She was hoping that outwardly her calm, casual demeanour had not shifted. In truth, she could feel the beads of perspiration snaking down her back.

It was stupid. She knew it was stupid. But the A and E department was different from the ward. There was something about the smell of these places. That mix of antiseptic and bleach that sent a tell-tale shiver down her spine. She was counting her breathing in her head, allowing herself to focus on the children around her, rather than let any memories sneak out from inside.

It was working, for the most part, just as long as no one accidentally put their hand on her back and felt the damp spot.

Gerry filmed as they watched the assessment of the little boy, Robbie, who'd fallen off his bike and stuck his hand out to save his fall. Rhuaridh's initial hunch had been correct. It was a fracture that was correctable with a cast and wouldn't require surgery. He even went as far as to relieve Pam in the plaster room and put on the blue fibreglass cast himself.

As he washed his hands and the others left the room, Kristie couldn't help but ask the question that was playing around in her head.

'Why are you being so nice this time?'

He gave a cough, which turned into a bit of a splutter. 'You mean I'm not always nice?'

She choked, and tried to cover that with a cough too. By the time her eyes met his he was actually smiling. He was teasing her.

She put one hand on her hip and tilted her head. 'Okay, so you obviously know that you haven't been. What gives?'

'What gives?'

She nodded and folded her hands over her chest. She couldn't help her distinctly American expressions. It wasn't as if he didn't use enough Scottish ones of his own. Half the time she felt as if he should come with a dictionary. 'What are you up to, and why have you decided to play nice?'

He finished drying his hands and turned to face her head on. Today he was dressed a little more casually. A short-sleeved striped casual shirt and a pair of jeans.

'Someone gave me a telling-off.'

'Who?' Now she was definitely curious.

'An older woman who came to the surgery this morning. She basically told me to behave. I haven't been told that since I was six.'

She shook her head. 'I don't believe that for a second.'

He paused for a second, as if he was trying to find the right words. 'We need to talk about what's been filmed—what it's right for you to show. But there's something else first.'

She'd just started to relax a little, but those words—'what it's right for you to show'—immediately raised her hackles. She didn't like anyone telling her what to do.

She couldn't help her short answer. 'What do you mean—what it's right for us to show?' Part of her brain knew the answer to this already. She'd had a few tiny reservations about the filming at John Henderson's house. But it had just felt too important—too big—to leave out.

She was automatically being defensive, even though she knew she might partly be in the wrong. She'd wanted to pick up the phone—not to ask his permission, just to give him a heads-up. But even though she hadn't done that, something inside her now just wouldn't let her back down. What was it with this guy? It was like he'd drawn her in, almost made her laugh, just so she might let her guard down a little then he could get into a fight with her.

The tone of her voice had obviously annoyed Rhuaridh. The smile dropped from his face and he straightened more. 'I haven't seen it,' he said sharply. 'But I'm not sure I approve of you showing film of John Henderson's death.

It seems...' a crease appeared in his brow as he tried to search for the correct word '...intrusive, unnecessary.' He shook his head. 'You didn't have the correct permissions.'

Every word seemed like a prickle on her skin. 'We got permission from Mr Henderson before we visited his home, *before* he died.'

She didn't mean to emphasise the word, but she was all fired up. And as soon as the words left her mouth she realised her mistake.

The look that passed over Rhuaridh's face was unmistakeable. Complete and utter guilt. It was almost like her mouth wouldn't stop working. It was like he'd questioned her integrity and her ethics. She wouldn't let anyone get away with that. Parts of her brain were telling her to stop and think, but her mouth wasn't paying any attention to those parts.

'And we shot everything from the back. You obscured the view of Mr Henderson. The only thing that was seen was his feet. Do you really think we'd show a poor dead man on the TV show?'

'You shouldn't have shown anything at all,' snapped Rhuaridh. 'You might have gained

John's permission, but to show him after he died, that's just ghoulish!'

She folded her arms across her chest. 'Don't you dare question the integrity of the show. You admitted yourself you haven't seen it—you don't even know the context in which the scenes were shown.'

'The integrity of the show? You showed a dead man!' His voice was getting louder.

'We didn't!' she shouted back. 'And you have no idea how the public reacted to it. They loved it. They didn't think it was ghoulish. They thought it was wonderful. Emotional. And sad. The whole purpose of this show is to show them something real. You can't get much more real than death.'

Those words seem to bubble up from somewhere unexpected inside her. They came out harshly, because that's what death was to her. She could remember every emotion, every thought, every feeling that had encompassed her when she'd been in that hospital room. All the things she'd been trying to keep locked in a box, deep down inside her.

For the briefest of seconds Rhuaridh looked a bit taken aback. But it seemed he was every bit as defensive as she was. 'Death is private. Death is something that shouldn't be shown in a TV show.' He stepped forward. 'If the same thing had happened to Magda's baby, would you show that too?'

His words almost took her breath away. It was the first time she'd stuttered since she'd been around him. 'W-what? N-no.' She shook her head fiercely. 'No. Of course not. What kind of people do you think we are?'

'The kind of people who intrude in others' lives, constantly looking for a story.'

An uncomfortable shiver shot down her spine. It was almost like Rhuaridh had been in the room with Louie when he'd been telling her to find a story, make a story, stir up a story to keep their part of the show the most popular. Now she was just cross.

'Why did you agree to do this anyway? You obviously don't want to be filmed. You couldn't make it any more apparent that you don't want us here. Haven't you ever watched any of the reality TV shows based in hospitals before? What did you actually expect to happen?'

He put his hand to his chest. '*I* didn't agree to this. Magda did. I had less than ten minutes' notice that you were coming. And I couldn't exactly say no, because my pregnant colleague had already signed the contract and negotiated a new X-ray machine for our department. So don't make the mistake that any of this was my idea. And what makes you think for a second I've watched any reality TV shows?' He almost spat those last words out.

The words burned her—as if what she was doing was ridiculous and worthless. Everything about this guy just seemed to rile her up in a way she'd never felt before. 'Do you think it's fun being around a guy all day who treats you like something on the bottom of their shoe?'

The A and E charge nurse, June, walked into the room. 'What on earth is going on in here? I could hear you guys at the bottom of the corridor. This is a hospital, not some kind of school playground.'

It was clear that June wasn't one to mince her words. Heat rushed into Kristie's cheeks. How humiliating. She opened her mouth to apologise but June had automatically turned on Rhuaridh.

'This isn't like you. Why on earth are you treating Kristie like this? She's only here doing a job and she spent most of yesterday on the ward talking to all the patients. They loved her. They want her to come back.'

Rhuaridh had the good grace to look embarrassed. He hung his head. It was almost odd seeing him like that, his hands on his hips and his gaze downward. He gave a low-voiced response. 'Sorry, June. We're having a bit of a difference of opinion.'

'I'll say you are. This is my A and E department and if you can't play nicely together I'll just separate you. Kristie? I hope you like kids. We've got a few in the room down the corridor who all need some kind of treatment— I've checked with the parents and you can film. Rhuaridh, I've got a potential case of appendicitis I need you to review and a couple of X-rays for you to look at.' She looked at them both. 'Now, hop to it. I've got a department to run.' June turned on her heel and strode back out the door.

For a few seconds there was silence—as if both of them were getting over their outbursts. Rhuaridh spoke first. 'You wouldn't guess she was the mother of twins, would you?'

It was so not what she'd expected to hear,

and unexpected laughter bubbled at the back of her throat.

It broke the tension in the room between them.

'I'm sorry,' he continued. 'I haven't been so hospitable and I know that. I guess I felt backed into a corner. This show isn't something I would have agreed to—certainly never have volunteered for. But I can't say no. The hospital needs the new X-ray machine. You can tell that alone just by the waiting room today.' He gave a slow shake of his head as the corners of his lips actually turned upwards. 'And you seem to have really bad timing.'

She let out a laugh. 'What?'

He kept shaking his head. 'I'm beginning to wonder if you're a jinx. First the thing with John Henderson, then the thing with Magda. You always seem to be around when there's a crisis.'

'You mean you never had any crises on Arran until we started filming?' She deliberately phrased the question so he'd realise he was being ridiculous.

He sighed. 'Of course we did. But believe it or not, lots of days are just normal stuff.

Nothing that dramatic or exciting, and to be honest…?' He looked away. 'I kind of like those days.'

Now she was curious. She'd done a little more research on Rhuaridh Gillespie since the last time she'd been here. She knew he'd taken over at his father's surgery when they couldn't recruit anyone to the post.

'I'm surprised to hear you say that. I thought you only came here because you had to.'

He looked up sharply, as if he hadn't expected her to know that. 'Recruitment is an issue right across the whole of Scotland. It used to be that for every GP vacancy there would be fifty applicants. Now young doctors just don't want to go into general practice. They don't want to have to own a business—run a business, and take on the huge financial debt of buying into a practice. If they even train to work as a general practitioner, they can make more money working as a locum. Then there's less pressure, less responsibility and…' he shook his head '…absolutely no continuity of care for patients.'

Kristie leaned back against the wall. 'But you trained as a general practitioner. Did you just want to work as a locum?'

He met her gaze with a thoughtful expression, as if he hadn't expected her to ask this many questions. 'I had alternative plans. At my practice in Glasgow I also worked a few days in one of the city hospitals in Dermatology. I covered outlying clinics across Glasgow, doing lots of minor surgery.'

Her mouth quirked upwards. 'You're a skin guy?'

He held out his hands. 'Biggest organ of the body. Why not?'

'And you can't do that here?'

He shrugged. 'Not as much. Sure, I can do biopsies, freeze moles with liquid nitrogen, or surgically remove anything small and suspicious. But when your population is usually around five thousand, that's not really enough people to only specialise in dermatology.'

She waited a few moments. 'So why didn't you just stay in Glasgow? Couldn't you just have left the practice here with only one doctor?'

Rhuaridh took a step back and leaned on the opposite wall. 'And leave Magda here on her own, covering the hospital and the GP practice? Leaving the community I grew up in and loved with no real service provision? What kind of person would that make me?'

It was like a bright light shining in her eyes. She could feel tiny pieces of the jigsaw puzzle slot into place.

Guilt. He'd felt responsible, and had come back to his home without really wanting to. This had a strange air of déjà vu about it. Wasn't this what had just happened with the TV series? He hadn't chosen to do this either, instead he was taking the place of his colleague unwillingly because he didn't want to let her, or the community, down. Kristie didn't doubt for one second that if he'd reneged on the contract, Arran would never get a new X-ray machine.

No wonder the guy was grumpy. Did he get to make any choices in this life?

She looked across the room into those weary blue eyes and said words she'd never have imagined herself saying. 'I guess it makes you a good person, Rhuaridh Gillespie.'

CHAPTER FOUR

August

MAC WAS LOOKING at him with an expression only a dog could give.

Rhuaridh bent down and rubbed his head. 'I'm sorry.' He meant it. He'd been neglectful. August was part of the summer season on Arran. From the end of June until the middle of August, Arran was full of Scottish, and lots of international, tourists. But come mid-August in Scotland the schools started again. Usually that would mean that things would quieten down.

But, in the UK, the English schools were still out. So, Arran was currently filled with lots of English holidaymakers. The beach had been packed all day. It seemed that croup was doing the rounds and between the surgery and the A and E department, he'd seen five toddlers with the nasty barking cough today alone. Chicken pox also seemed to be rearing its head again.

Five members of one poor family were currently covered in the itchy spots.

He glanced at his watch. Kristie was due to arrive at some point and he was feeling quite… awkward.

He wasn't quite sure what had come over him last time around, and he had apologised to her, but they still had nine months of filming left. He counted in days. Twenty-seven more days around Kristie Nelson.

There was something about her. At first he'd thought it was the accent and the confidence. But he'd seen her waver on a few occasions. Her confidence was only skin deep. And that was another thing. To others, she may look like a typical anchor woman for an American TV show. Blonde, perfect teeth, hint of a tan and good figure. And somehow he couldn't help watching the way she flicked her thumb off her forefinger, or made that little clicking noise when she was thinking. It was weird. Even though he told himself she was the most annoying female on the planet, he couldn't help the way his mind would frequently drift back to something she'd said or done.

Mac nuzzled around his ankles. It snapped him back from the Kristie fog and he picked up Mac's lead and grabbed his sweater. 'Let's go, boy.' He opened the main door of his cottage and Mac bounded out towards the beach. He'd adjusted well to the move, and after a few short months it actually felt like Mac had always been there. He'd even employed a dog walker to take Mac out during the day when he was working.

The sun was dipping in the sky, leaving the beach scattered with violet evening hues. There were a few other people walking dogs, someone on a horse and a couple strolling along hand in hand.

The breeze tonight wasn't quite as brisk as it normally was. Laughter carried along the beach in the air. A group of teenagers was trying to set up a campfire.

Rhuaridh moved down closer to the firmer sand at the sea's edge. The beach ran for a few miles and Mac had got used to a long walk in the evening.

They'd only been walking for about ten minutes when he heard thudding feet behind him.

He turned to take a step one way or the other and Kristie ran straight into him.

'Oh! Wow.' She stepped back and rubbed her nose.

He laughed and shook his head. 'Where did you come from?'

She was still rubbing her nose. 'I came by your house. I wanted to chat to you about the schedule tomorrow.'

'You came by my house? I wasn't expecting to see you until tomorrow.' He was surprised. He hadn't known Kristie knew where he lived—and after their last meeting, he was even more surprised she wanted to turn up at his door.

She nodded. 'We ended up swapping flights and coming a day early.'

'Does that mean you're going home a day early?'

She let out a laugh. 'Don't even try to pretend you want me around, then.'

'No.' He cringed. 'I didn't mean it like that. I'm just wondering if you wanted to swap things around.'

She stopped for a second, bending down to pat Mac, who'd bounded back to see why Rhuaridh had stopped walking. 'Hey, guy, nice to see you.'

Mac jumped up, putting two wet sandy paw-prints on her jeans. He would have expected her to squirm but Kristie didn't seem bothered at all. She crouched down, letting Mac lick her hands. Kristie looked up at him. 'I thought we should maybe have a chat,' she said, biting her bottom lip.

A heavy feeling settled in his stomach. 'About last time? Yeah, we probably should.'

Her nose wrinkled. 'Not about last time,' she said. 'I thought we sorted that.'

Now he was really confused. 'Well, yeah, we sort of did, but…' He wasn't quite sure what to say next.

She straightened up, wiping her wet hands on her jeans. 'I wanted to talk to you about some-thing else.'

'Okay.' He wasn't quite sure where this was going.

She sucked in a breath, not quite meeting his gaze. 'Let's walk.' She turned and started in the same direction he'd been headed.

'Okay,' he said again, wondering what he was getting himself into.

'You said you hadn't watched the show.'

He shook his head. 'Not my thing—no offence.'

She gave a smile, then stuck her hands in her pockets and turned to face him again. The setting sun outlined her silhouette and streaked her blonde hair with violet and pink light—like some kind of ethereal hue.

'None taken.' She cleared her throat. 'I thought I should probably let you know something.'

'What?'

'I watched the third episode before I came here. It goes out in two weeks' time.'

'And…?' He knew there must be something, why else would they be having this conversation?

She reached up and tugged at her earlobe. A sign she was nervous. He was noticing all these little things about her. Now he knew when she was angry, when she was thinking, and when she was nervous. How many other women did he know those things about?

Had he known them about his ex, Zoe? He couldn't even remember. All his memories of her had just seemed to fade into the past.

Her words came out rushed, as if she was trying to say them all before she could stop herself. 'The show's been really popular. Really popular. Partly because in the first episode it covered John Henderson's death, and in the second it introduced a beautiful baby into the world.'

He wrinkled his nose. He was thinking back to the last time she'd been here. No major events had happened.

'So what's wrong with the third episode? Not enough drama?'

She looked distinctly uncomfortable and fixed her gaze on the teenagers further down the beach. 'Nothing's wrong with it exactly. It's just changed focus a little.'

'Changed focus to what?' He was getting tired with this tiptoeing around. 'Why don't you just say what you need to?'

She pressed her lips together for a second. 'The fight we had? Gerry filmed it. He'd already captured us sparring a little in the episodes before and people had been commenting on social media about it.'

Rhuaridh's brain flashed back to the woman in the surgery, telling him he had to be nicer to Kristie. He groaned. 'Oh, no. I look like a complete and utter—'

She held up her hand and stopped him. 'My producer says it's dynamite. He says everyone is going to love it.'

'They'll love you.' Rhuaridh shook his head. 'I'm the villain. I'm the one who lost his patience.'

He could see her biting the inside of her lip.

'I'm sorry,' he said quickly.

'Don't be,' she said, equally quickly. 'The last few shows I've worked on have all been cancelled. I was beginning to be a bit of bad luck charm. In TV, that kind of reputation doesn't do you any favours.'

He stuck his hands into his pockets. 'So, you want to fight with me? Is that what you're saying?'

She pulled a face and gave a little shrug. 'Well…yes and no. It seems that a bit of tension is good for viewing—alongside all the medical stuff, of course.'

'I'm not sure fighting on screen does much for me as a doctor. I'm not normally like that.'

She gave a weak smile. 'So it's just me that drives you nuts?'

He looked out over the sea. This was the first time they'd really talked. How did he explain she might be right, without offending her—because if he couldn't understand it, how could she?

'I guess I still need to get used to someone following me around,' he said carefully. 'What are the other shows in the series?' It was a blatant attempt at changing the subject. But he was beginning to think he should have paid more attention to all the TV stuff.

'There's a museum curator in Egypt—apparently she practically doesn't let them into any room that hosts an "artefact", and the guy who is training to be an astronaut is said to be a major jerk. After the first shows they brought in someone new to follow—a guy who's trying to make his name as a country and western singer. I'm reliably informed that his singing is the worst ever heard.'

He couldn't help but laugh again. His foot traced a line in the sand. Mac had long since tired of waiting around for them both and was now chasing the tide, getting his white and black coat well and truly soaked. The smell of wet dog was going to drift all the way through the house.

'I can't imagine what they find so exciting about a doctor on an island in Scotland.'

'Maybe it's the exotic. Half the world just wants to visit Scotland and this makes them feel like they've been there.' She gave him a sideways glance. 'Or maybe they just like the grumpy doc.'

The grumpy doc. Was that what she'd nicknamed him? It wasn't the most flattering description in the world. His stomach twisted a little. He should be worrying about his reputation. He should be worrying about what people might think of him. But, strangely, the only person's opinion he was worried about right now was Kristie's. 'Why are you telling me all this?'

'I know you don't watch the series. But I thought I should forewarn you—in case, once the next episode hits, you start to get some press.'

'Bad press, you mean.'

She gave him a smile. 'Actually, no. I've told you. They love you. I was thinking more along

the lines that you might get weird internet pro-
posals, or your dating profile might explode.'

'My dating profile? You honestly think I've
got a dating profile?'

She held out her hands and gave him a mis-
chievous smile. 'Who knows?'

He shook his head as they started back down
the beach. 'On an island this small I pretty
much know everyone. If I had a dating profile, the whole island would know it, and anyway it's a bit hard to meet for dates when you
rely on a ferry to the mainland.'

He looked at her curiously. 'Do you have
one—a dating profile?'

She threw back her head and laughed. 'Are
you joking? I was on TV for about ten seconds
before I started getting weird emails. It seems
that being on a TV show makes you fair game.
Nope. I just try to meet guys the old-fashioned
way.'

He looked down at her as they walked side
by side. 'And how's that working out for you?'
He couldn't pretend he wasn't curious.

She gave him an oblique glance. She knew.
She knew the question he was asking. She held
out her hand and wiggled it. 'Hmm...'

What did that mean?

She didn't say anything else so he was kind of left hanging.

'So, is everything okay for tomorrow, then?'

He nodded. 'Sure.' At that moment Mac ran up and decided to shake half of the Firth of Clyde all over them.

'Whoa!' Both of them jumped back, laughing, Kristie wiping the huge drops of water from her face and neck.

Rhuaridh took a step closer. 'Sorry.' He looked towards Mac. 'Occupational hazard, I guess.'

He reached forward without thinking. Part of her mascara had smudged just under her lower eyelid. He lifted his thumb to her cheekbone and wiped it away. Her laughter stopped as she looked up, her gaze connecting with his.

His hand froze. It was like all the breath had just been sucked from his lungs. He was so conscious of the feel of her smooth skin beneath his thumb pad. He could almost swear a tiny little zing shot down his arm.

She wasn't moving either. Her pupils dilated as he watched.

It was like every sense inside him switched on. He hadn't been paying attention. He'd been so focused on his work he'd forgotten to see what was right beside him. When was the last time he'd actually dated? Maybe once in the ten months since he'd got here. He couldn't even remember.

He couldn't remember what it was like to let a woman's scent drift around him like it was now. To look into a pair of eyes that were looking right back at him.

There was a shout behind them and both of them jumped back. It was only one of the teenagers carrying on.

But the moment was gone. Kristie looked a little embarrassed and wiped her hands down on her jeans. 'I'd better get back,' she said quickly. 'Gerry and I need to chat about the filming tomorrow.' She started to walk quickly down the beach, then turned once to look at him. 'I'll see you tomorrow.'

The words seem to hang between them, as if she was willing him to add something else. But he gave a quick nod. 'Sure.'

Kristie broke into a jog back down the beach. He couldn't help but stare at her silhouette. Mac bounded up and sat at his feet, looking up at him quizzically.

If there was mental telepathy between a human and a dog, Mac was currently calling him an idiot.

He kicked the sand at his feet. 'I know, I know,' he said as he shook his head and stuck his hands in his pockets.

He pushed his thoughts from his head. She was from LA. She worked on a TV show. He was crazy to think she might actually be interested in some guy from Arran. His ex had been quick to tell him that Arran was a dull, boring rock in the middle of nowhere. What could it possibly have to interest some woman who was probably two minutes from Hollywood? He stared out as the sun drew even closer to the horizon, sending warming streaks across the sky. He sighed. 'Let's go, Mac,' he said as he turned and headed back to the cottage.

Kristie dressed carefully. For the first time since she'd come to the island she wore a dress. It was still summer here—even though it was much cooler than LA. Her hair didn't usually give her much trouble, so she just ran a brush through it as usual. Her makeup took her no more than five minutes. She'd even applied it once in a dark cupboard with no light.

Gerry gave her a smile as she emerged from her room in their rental. 'Special occasion?'

She shook her head, and pretended she didn't notice the rush of heat to her cheeks. What on earth was she doing? Maybe she'd just imagined that moment on the beach. Maybe it had been nothing at all. She'd only wanted to warn him about the hype. Or had she?

Truth was, she never really watched herself on TV much. It seemed too egotistical. But watching the episode between her and Rhuaridh had brought all those emotions back to the surface. She couldn't ever remember a guy getting under her skin the way Rhuaridh Gillespie had. And on the way over on the ferry this time she'd been nervous. Something else that was unusual for her.

Maybe it was the apparent popularity of the show. She'd already had a few interview requests. Last night when she'd logged onto her social media account she'd seen over four hundred comments about the show. What would happen when the third show went out?

Gerry was leaning against the wall. He looked paler than normal. 'Okay?' she asked.

'Sure,' he said. 'Just a bit of indigestion. It's my age.'

She gave a nod and headed to the stairs. They were filming at the surgery today, covering one of the paediatric clinics and immunisation clinics.

Screaming babies. Just her kind of thing. Not.

Gerry fumbled in his pocket and some lollipops landed on the floor. Kristie bent and picked them up. 'Since when did you like candy?'

He tapped the side of his nose. 'It's my secret weapon. It's in case we have unco-operative kids at the clinic today.'

She shook her head and held up one of the bright red lollipops. 'It's a pure sugar rush. No way will they let you hand these out. Think of the tooth decay.'

He winked. 'I'm wiser than you think. They're sugar-free.' He started walking down the stairs in front of her. 'Don't let it be said that an old guy doesn't have any new tricks.'

'What about the additives?' She stared at the colour again.

He shrugged in front of her. 'Can't think of everything.'

She shook her head and stuck some in the pocket of her dress. She could always eat them herself.

The clinic was chaos. It was a mixture of development checks, immunisations and childhood reviews.

Most of the mothers were delighted at the prospect of their child being filmed, so permissions were easy.

Rhuaridh was wearing a pale pink shirt today and dark trousers. She hated the fact he always looked so handsome. He moved through the waiting room easily, picking up babies and toddlers and carrying them through to the examination room, all while chatting to their mothers. He seemed at ease here. It was as if he'd finally decided to accept they'd be around and was doing what they'd asked him to do right from the beginning—ignore them.

But it made Kristie's insides twist in a way she didn't like.

Some of babies squealed. She didn't blame them, getting three jabs at once was tough. She didn't have much experience around kids or babies, so watching Ellen, the health visitor, do the development checks was more interesting than she'd thought.

She watched the babies follow things with their eyes, weight bear on their legs, and lift their heads up in line with their bodies. The older ones could grab things, sit up and balance on their own, and babble away quite happily.

Her favourite was a little boy just short of two years old. He came into the room with the biggest frown on his face. When Ellen tried to persuade him to build some bricks, say a few words or draw with a crayon he had the same response to everything. 'No.' His mother looked tired and sat with another baby on her lap, apologising profusely for her son's lack of co-operation.

Ellen took some measurements and laughed and turned to Kristie. 'As you can see, he has a younger sister. I've been in the house a dozen times and know he can do all these things—if he wants to.'

Kristie stopped smiling at the little guy and turned her attention to the mum. She had dark circles under her eyes and looked as if she might burst into tears. Kristie's first reaction was to open her mouth and move into counselling mode but before she could, Ellen gave an almost imperceptible nod of her head towards Kristie and Gerry, and they backed out of the room.

Kristie stood against the wall for a few minutes and just breathed. She had no idea what was going on with that woman, but her own thoughts immediately raced back to her sister. The last few volunteer shifts on the helpline had been quiet. She'd almost willed the phone to ring, then had felt guilty for thinking that. In the end, she'd used the time in an unexpected way.

She'd started writing. She wasn't sure what it was at first, but it had started to take shape into a piece of fiction—a novel, based on her experience with her sister and how suicide affected everyone. Her sister's death had impacted on every part of her life. She'd watched the life drain from her mother and father and their health deteriorate quickly, with them eventually dying within a few months of each other.

Burying three family members in a short period of time had messed with her head so much she found it hard to form new relationships. Hard to find hope to invest in a future that might get snatched away from her. Of course, thoughts like those were irrational. She knew that. But she also knew that the last few men she'd met she'd kept at arm's length. Whether she'd wanted to or not.

She sighed as the door opened again and Ellen crossed the hall to Rhuaridh's room with a slip of paper in her hand.

Kristie's mouth dried as the health visitor took charge of the children, then let the mother go and see Rhuaridh on her own.

She couldn't help herself but follow Ellen to where she was bouncing the baby on her knee and entertaining the toddler, who'd now decided to draw pictures.

'Is she okay?'

Ellen looked up. 'It's likely she has postnatal depression. We screen all new mums twice in the first year. I've visited Jackie at home a lot. She's had two very colicky babies. Lack of sleep is tough.'

Kristie rubbed her hands up and down her arms, instantly cold. That piece of paper. That assessment that they do on all new mums— why hadn't there been something like that for her sister? Would it have worked? Would it have picked anything up?

Maybe she was putting hope in something that didn't exist. But just the thought—that there was a simple screening tool that would have picked up something...

'Do you use it for other people?'

Ellen looked up. She'd started building a pile of bricks on the floor with the toddler. 'The postnatal depression scale? No, it's designed specifically for women who've just had a baby. We've used it for years, though, and I think it's very effective. Even if it just starts a conversation between me and the mum.'

'But you took her through to see Rhuaridh?'

Ellen looked over Kristie's shoulder. 'This is very personal. I have to ask that you don't film anything about this case.'

Kristie nodded. 'Of course not.'

'In that case, the final question in the tool—it's about self-harm. It asks if the mum has ever felt that way. If she answers anything other than no, I always need to have a conversation with the GP.'

Kristie felt her voice shake. 'So, what do you do for mums who feel like that?'

Ellen gave her a thoughtful look. 'It all depends on the mum. Some I visit more, every day if I have to. Some I get some other support—like a few hours at nursery for one, or both of their kids. Some Rhuaridh will see. He might decide to start them on some medication, or to refer them to the community mental health nurse, or even to a consultant. Whatever will help the mum most.'

Kristie leaned back against the wall, taking in everything that was being said. The mum was in with Rhuaridh for a while. By the time she came out, she was wiping her eyes but seemed a bit better. It was as if a little spark had appeared in her eyes again. Maybe she finally felt as if someone was listening.

Kristie waited until the clinic was finished then found Rhuaridh while he was writing up some notes.

'That mum? What did you do for her?'

He looked a little surprised by her question but gestured for her to close the door. 'Sit down,' he said.

She took a deep breath and sat down on the chair next to him. 'I talked to her,' he said quietly.

'That's it?' She couldn't hide how taken aback she felt.

'And I listened,' he added.

'But her questionnaire...' she began.

He held up his hand. 'Her questionnaire is just a little bit of her. It's a snapshot in time. I listened. I listened to how she was feeling and talked to her and let her know that some of this is normal for a new mum. She's beyond tired. She hasn't had a full night's sleep in two years. How do you think that would impact on anyone's mental health?'

'But you let her leave...' Her voice trailed off, as her mind jumped ahead.

'I let her leave with an assurance of some support systems in place. While she was here, she phoned her sister and asked her to take the kids overnight. She's coming back to see me again tomorrow and we'll talk again.'

'Oh.' Kristie sagged into the chair a little. Her stomach still churned.

There was so much here that was tumbling around in her brain. She knew that most of the thoughts she was having weren't rational—they were all tinged by her own experience. That desperate sense of panic.

She took a few breaths and tried to put her counselling head on. The one she used three nights a month. Rhuaridh had taken time to talk to the mother and acknowledge her feelings—usually the single most important act someone could do. Then he'd arranged follow up and support. Just like she would hope and expect from a health professional.

Rhuaridh leaned forward and put his hand over hers. 'Kristie, is everything all right?'

And for the first time in her life she wasn't quite sure how to answer. Should she tell him? Should she let him know she worked as a counsellor and what she'd been through herself?

Her mouth was dry. He was looking at her with those bright blue eyes—staring right at her as though he could see right down to her very soul. To all the things she kept locked away tight. Part of her wanted to tell him. Part of her wanted to share.

But something was stopping her. Something wouldn't let her open her mouth and say those words. So before she could think about it any longer, she got up and rushed out.

CHAPTER FIVE

September

'YOU'VE NEVER WATCHED?'

Rhuaridh shook his head as Magda cradled baby Alice. She gave him a curious smile. 'I can't believe it. You should. I have to admit, I'm almost a little jealous.'

'Of what?'

He was drinking a large cup of coffee while he compared a few notes with her on a few of their chronically ill patients. On Arran, a doctor would never really be off duty, and Magda was far too nosy not to want to discuss some of their long-term cases.

'Of you.' She waved one hand while she fixed her gaze back on her fair-haired daughter while she screwed up her nose and gave a sigh. 'But no. If I'd been in the show that wouldn't have worked anyway.'

Rhuaridh put down his cup and held out his

hands. 'Give me my goddaughter and tell me what on earth you're talking about.'

Magda stood up and put Alice into his arms, before settling back and putting her feet up on the sofa. 'It's all about the chemistry.'

'Chemistry? I thought you didn't like chemistry. You always complained about it when we were students.'

She shook her head and looked at him as if he was completely dumb. 'Not school chemistry. *Chemistry*. You know…between a man and a woman. Phew! If I need to teach you about the birds and bees I'm going to question whether you should be working as a doctor.'

He shifted in the chair, realising where this was going to go. He shook his head and Alice wrinkled her face. He stopped moving. He knew who was in charge here.

He spoke quietly. 'I've no interest in watching myself on TV. I know everything that's happened—not all of which I'm entirely proud of.'

She gave a sigh. 'You know. They edit things. And they've edited the show for the drama. To be honest, I'm surprised we've not got women heading to Arran by the boatload.' She raised one eyebrow. 'They always seem to catch your good side.'

'Do I have a bad side?' he teased.

But it was almost as if Magda was still talking to herself. 'Then again, most of the women would know they wouldn't get a look in. The chemistry between you and Kristie...' she kissed her fingertips then flicked out her fingers '...is just off the scale.' She gave him a smile. 'You're doing so much better than the others in the show. I can't even watch the country and western singer. And the astronaut is possibly the most arrogant person on and off the planet.'

His mind was spinning. Was everyone who was watching thinking the same thing about him and Kristie? He felt like some teenage boy under scrutiny. *He* hadn't even really worked out what was going on between them.

He liked her. He knew he liked her. But anything more just seemed...ridiculous.

But was it?

Alice made a little noise in his arms. Magda closed her eyes. 'She didn't sleep a wink last night.'

'Didn't she?'

Rhuaridh looked around and glimpsed the pram near the doorway. 'Do you want me to take her for a walk? Mac is mooching around outside anyway. I was planning on taking him for a walk.'

'Would you?' As she said the words she snuggled down further into the sofa. 'Just an hour would be great.'

Rhuaridh smiled and settled Alice into the pram, closing the door as quietly as he could behind him.

Mac gave him a look. Rhuaridh wagged his finger. 'Don't get jealous, old one. Just get in line. We've got a new boss now.'

'Really?'

Rhuaridh nearly jumped. Kristie was standing behind him with a bag in her hand.

'Where did you come from?'

She grinned. 'LA. You know, America.' She made signals with her hands. 'Then a plane and a boat.'

'Okay, okay, I get it.'

She was wearing a pair of black and white checked trousers and a black shirt tied at her waist. Her hair was loose about her shoulders and she seemed totally at ease as she leaned over him and looked into the pram. 'I came to see my favourite girl, but I see you've already kidnapped her. Whaddya say we share?'

Rhuaridh gripped the pram a little tighter as he smiled back. 'Ah, but this is my goddaughter. And this is the first time I've actually managed to kidnap her.'

Kristie made the little clicking noise she always did when she was thinking. He leaned a little closer and caught a whiff of her light zesty perfume. 'To tell you the truth, I think Mac's a little jealous.'

Kristie dropped to her knees and rubbed Mac's head, bending down to put her head next to his. 'Poor boy. Is he neglecting you again?' She wrapped her hand around Mac's lead. 'How about we take turns? I'll take Mac, then swap you on the way back.'

Rhuaridh gave a nod and they started to walk down towards the town. The weather was bright with just a little edge in the air. Kristie chatted constantly, telling him about plane delays and double-booked accommodation. It didn't take long for her to turn the conversation back to work. 'Have you seen that young mum again?'

Rhuaridh gave her a sideways glance. Last

time he'd seen Kristie she'd been more than a little preoccupied about the case. She'd rushed out the room when he'd asked her if something was wrong, and the next day she'd left to go back to LA. He hadn't seen her since.

He'd been curious about why she'd been so concerned. He'd had enough experience in life to know when to tread carefully. People didn't come with a label attached declaring their past life experiences.

'I've seen her quite a lot—so has Ellen, the health visitor. She's talking, and I don't think she's going to feel better overnight, but I think if we have adequate support systems in place, and an open-door policy, I think she'll continue to make improvements. Ellen has visited her at home a lot—talked through how she's feeling about things. They've even been out walking together—like we are today.'

He gave her another glance. He thought he knew what the next answer would be. 'You haven't included anything in the filming, have you?'

Kristie shook her head. 'Absolutely not. It's mainly just footage from the immunisation clinic and the baby clinic.'

He gave a nod and then changed tack. 'So, what are you and Gerry going to do tonight about food?'

She blinked. 'What do you mean?'

'The place you've booked into after the mix up—they didn't tell you, did they? Their kitchen is out of order. Something to do with an electricity short.'

Kristie let out a big sigh. 'Darn it. I never even asked. We just said we needed beds for the next few days after the mix-up at the other place.'

She nudged him as they kept walking. 'Okay, so give me the lowdown on all the local places.' She wrinkled her nose. 'Though I'm not sure about Gerry. He's been really tired. I think the jet-lag is hitting him hard this time.'

Rhuaridh gave her a cheeky kind of grin. 'Well, if you can promise me that you actually eat, I'll show you my favourite place in town.'

'What do you mean—if I actually eat?'

He laughed. 'You're from LA. Don't you all just eat green leaves and the occasional bit of kale or spinach?'

Now she laughed too. 'You heard about that

new diet?' She shuddered. 'Oh, no. Not for me. Anyhow, I'm a steak kind of girl.'

'You are?' He actually stopped walking and looked at her in surprise.

She pointed to her chest. 'What? I don't look like a steak girl?'

He couldn't help but give her an appreciative gaze. 'If steak's what you like, I know just the place.'

She glanced around. They were right in the heart of Brodick now. There were a number of shops on the high street, a sprinkling of coffee shops and a few pubs.

'Cool. Which one is it?'

He turned the pram around. 'It's back this way.'

Quick as a flash, Kristie came alongside and bumped him out of the way with her hip, taking his place at pushing the pram. 'Don't try and steal my turn. You got the way out. I get the way back.' She bent over the pram and stroked the side of Alice's face. 'She's just a little jewel, isn't she?'

He was surprised at the affection in her voice. 'You like kids?'

'I love kids.' She shrugged. 'Not all of them like me, right enough.'

He stopped walking. 'Where did you pick that up?'

'What?' There was a gleam in her eye.

'"Right enough". It's a distinctly Scottish expression.'

She lifted one hand from the pram and counted off on her fingers. 'I was trying it out for size. Everyone uses it in the surgery. I'm also looking for opportunities to use *drookit*, *minging* and...' She wrinkled her brow. 'What's the one that Mr McLean who comes to the surgery always uses?'

Rhuaridh burst out laughing. 'Wheesht?'

'That's it!' she said, pointing her finger at him. *'Wheesht.'*

It sounded strange in her American accent. But he liked it. He liked it a lot.

She started walking again. 'There's another one I've heard. It might even be used to describe you sometimes.' She gave him a nod of her head.

'I dread to think. Hit me with it.'

This time the glance she gave him was part

mysterious, part superior. 'Crabbit,' she said triumphantly.

Part of him was indignant, part of him wanted to laugh. 'Crabbit? Me?' He pointed to his chest. 'No way. No way could I ever be described as crabbit. I'm the nice guy. The fun-loving squishy kind of guy.' He gestured down to Alice. 'The kind of guy who takes his god-daughter for a walk to give his friend a break.' He raised his eyebrows at her. 'Beat that one, LA girl.'

She folded her arms across her chest, letting momentum carry the pram for a few seconds. 'That sounds like a challenge.'

'It is.' He'd never been one to back down from a challenge.

He swooped in and grabbed the pram handle. 'Ms Nelson, I believe you just neglected your duty. I think I should take over again.'

Before she could protest he nodded towards the pub at the other side of the road. 'Billy's Bar. Best steaks in town. They even do a special sauce for me.'

'What kind of sauce?'

'I could tell you. But I'd have to kill you. It's a secret I'll take to my grave. But if you come along with me tonight, I'll let you have some.' The words were out before he really had a chance to think about them.

'Dinner with the doctor,' she mused out loud. 'Just exactly how good are these steaks?'

'Better than you've ever tasted. The cows bred in the Arran hills are special. More tender.'

There was a smile dancing across her lips. 'Okay, then.' She gave him a cheeky wink. 'But only because I might want to put the steak on film.'

Part of him was elated. Part of him was put out. It had been a casual, not-really-thought-about invitation. But things had seemed to be heading in this direction. But now, had she only said yes because she wanted to film their dinner? Was this something to try and get more viewing figures?

Because that hadn't even crossed his mind.

Kristie kept chatting again. It seemed she had a gift for chat. And she didn't seem to slow down for a second. They were almost back at Magda's house when Rhuaridh's page sounded.

He took one glance and grabbed his phone.

'Something wrong?' she asked, taking over the pram-pushing again.

He nodded. Listened carefully to the person at the end of the phone before cutting the call. In the blink of an eye he swooped up little Alice, dropping a kiss on her forehead before running inside with her. Kristie was still fumbling with the pram in the doorway as he came back outside.

'Leave it,' he said, running past her. 'And phone Gerry. Tell him to meet us at the wilderness centre.'

Kristie's head flicked one way then the other, as if she should work out what to do next. He was in the car already and, reaching over, flung open the passenger door. 'Now, Kristie!' he yelled.

Her hands were refusing to do what they were told as she tried to phone Gerry. It took three attempts to finally press the correct button. Rhuaridh was driving quicker than she'd ever seen him. He'd already phoned the cottage hospital and given some instructions to the staff.

It seemed that there was only one ambulance on Arran and it was on its way too.

'What's the wilderness centre?'

'It's an experiential learning place. Adults and kids come and learn to mountain climb, hike, swim, canoe, camp, fish and a whole host of other things.'

'So…' She was almost scared to ask. 'What's happened?'

'There's been an accident. There's a waterfall in the hills. One of the instructors and one of the kids have been hurt.'

He turned up a track that led up one of the nearby hills. Now she understood why he had a four-wheel drive. The terrain was rugged. 'Will the ambulance get up here?'

He nodded. 'You haven't seen it yet, have you?'

She shook her head.

'It's not a regular ambulance because of the terrain it has to cover, well, that and the fact a high number of our injuries are around the foot of Goat Fell—'

'Goat Fell?' she interrupted.

He pointed off to the side. 'Arran's highest mountain, more than eight hundred metres tall. Really, really popular with climbers, and it is a real climb. Especially at the end. Some people don't really come equipped for it and end up injuring themselves.'

'Okay,' she murmured. She looked to where he pointed. She couldn't even see the top of the mountain as it was covered with low-hanging clouds.

They were climbing higher, going through trees and bushes. 'Where is this place?'

'Another few minutes.' He gave her an anxious kind of glance, his voice steady. 'Until the ambulance gets here you might need to give me a hand. Are you okay with that?'

Her response was quicker than he expected. 'It's only hospitals that spook me.'

'What?'

He caught one quick glimpse of her face before he had to look back at the path. For a split second he thought she might be cracking a joke, but her expression told him otherwise.

He swore he could see the pathways firing in his own brain. He'd thought she'd been a little unsettled in the hospital. Just something off— something he couldn't quite put his finger on.

'Why are you spooked by hospitals?'

It was totally not the right time to ask a question like that. And speeding up a hill towards an accident scene was not the right place to give an answer. Of course he knew that. But how could she expect him not to ask?

'Past experience,' she replied in a tight voice. 'One I'd rather not talk about.'

He couldn't help his response. 'You must have loved the thought of coming here.'

They reached the crest of the hill and veered down towards the valley where the waterfall lay.

She shot him a wry expression. 'Let's just say I really wanted the museum in Egypt or the astronaut. Lucky old me.'

His gut gave a twist. As they approached the waterfall site he could see an array of people, all dressed in wet-weather gear, crowded around a man on the ground.

He had to let this go right now. He had a job to do.

'Will you be okay to help?' he asked again. For the next few minutes at least he might need to count on Kristie for help. If she couldn't help, she might well be a hindrance and he'd ask her to stay in the car.

Her voice was tight and she glanced at her

phone. He reached over and grabbed her hand. 'Be honest.'

She stared for the briefest of seconds at his hand squeezing hers. 'I'll be fine,' she said without meeting his gaze. 'Gerry's messaged. He's just behind us. He was at the hospital and hitched a ride in the ambulance.'

Rhuaridh nodded. He had to take her at her word. He had to trust her. And hopefully it would only be for a few minutes.

'I'll grab the blue bag, you grab the red,' he said as he jumped from the car.

He walked swiftly to the group of people. One of the instructors was on the ground with a large laceration on his head. From one glance Rhuaridh could see that his breathing was a little laboured. But that was the point. At least he was breathing.

'Where's the other casualty?'

A teenage boy pointed to the bottom of the roaring waterfall. 'Under there. He jumped from the top.'

Rhuaridh's heart gave a little leap. 'Under *there*?'

'Not under the water. Under the waterfall. He

says he can't feel his legs so no one wanted to move him.'

Rhuaridh was already stripping off his shoes and jacket. He pulled a monitor from one bag, bent over and stuck the three leads on the first guy's chest. It only took a few seconds to check the readings. He knelt down beside the guy, pulled his stethoscope out and made another check. Lungs were filling normally, no sign of damage. 'What happened?' he asked the nearest kid.

'Ross and Des went into the water as soon as Kai jumped and went under. Des got Kai and pulled him into the cave but when Ross tried to climb the rock face he slipped and hit his head on the way down.' The young boy talking gulped, 'A few of us jumped in and pulled him out. He hasn't woken up at all.'

Rhuaridh pulled a penlight from his pocket and checked Ross's pupils, then completed a first set of neuro obs. It was first-line assessment for any head injury. He scribbled them down and handed them to Kristie.

He handed Kristie a radio. 'You keep these.'

'Where are you going?' There was a definite flash of panic in her eyes.

A teenage girl, her face streaked with tears, tugged at his sleeve. 'The other instructor is with Kai. He stayed with him after Ross got hurt, trying to help.'

Rhuaridh started rummaging through the kit-bags. He tucked the other radio into his belt. There was no doubt about it—he was going to get very wet.

He bent over next to Kristie, checking the monitor again. He kept his voice low. 'Keep an eye on his breathing. It seems fine and his heart rate is steady. He's given himself quite a bang on the head. If he starts to wake up, just keep him steady on the ground. If he's agitated or confused, radio me straight away.'

Rhuaridh wouldn't normally leave an uncon-scious patient, but right now he'd no idea of the condition of the child under the waterfall. As the only medic on site he had to assess both patients. He put his hand on Kristie's shoul-der. 'The ambulance crew should be here in a few minutes.' He could tell she was nervous, but she lifted her own hand and put it over his.

'Go on, Rhuaridh. Go and check on the kid. We'll be fine.'

Rhuaridh gave a few instructions to some of

the other teenagers around. Most were quiet, a few looked a bit shocked but had no injuries. 'Stay with Kristie, she'll let me know if there's any problems.'

He waded into the water. Cold. It was beyond cold. This waterfall was notorious for the temperature as it was based in a valley with little sunlight. By the time he'd waded across to the middle of the pool the water had come up over his waist and to the bottom of his ribs, making him catch his breath.

The instructor had been wearing a wetsuit that would keep his temperature more steady—hopefully the teenager would be too.

The spray from the waterfall started to soak him. He knew this place well enough. There was a ridge on the rocks the falls plummeted over. It was the only way to get access to the cave under the falls and the only way to access that ridge was to wade through the water and try and scale the rock face.

He had nothing. No climbing equipment. No wetsuit. Not even a rope.

He heard a painful groan. Even though the noise from the falls was loud, he could hear it echoing from the cave. He moved sideways, casting his eyes over the rock face, looking for a suitable place to start.

It had been years since he'd been here. As a teenager he'd been able to scale this rock with no problems. It had practically been a rite of passage for any kid that lived on the island. But that had been a long time ago, when he'd probably been a lot more agile than he was now.

The first foothold was easy, his bare foot pushing him upwards. He caught his hands on the rocks above and pulled himself up, finding a position for the second foot.

'Careful, Doc,' shouted one of the kids.

He moved left, nearer the falls. There was a trick to this, trying to keep hold of the wall, which got more and more slippery by the second as he edged closer. The weight on his back from the backpack and red portable stretcher was affecting his balance, making him grip all the tighter. His knuckles were white as he waited for the right second to duck his head and jump through the falls to the cave behind.

As he jumped he had a millisecond of panic. What if the injured kid was directly in his path? But as he landed with a grunt behind the falls he realised he was clear. He fell roughly to the side, the equipment on his back digging sharply into him.

It took his eyes a few seconds to adjust. It wasn't quite dark in here. Light still streamed through the waterfall.

'About time,' said Des, the instructor, cheekily. He was sitting next to the injured boy, who was lying on the floor of the cave.

The cave was larger than most people would expect, and the grey rock had streaks of brown and red. There was almost room for a person to stand completely upright, and definitely enough room for six or seven people to sit within the cave. This place had been one of the most popular hideouts when Rhuaridh had been a kid and half the island had scraped their initials into the rock. He'd half a mind to flash his torch over the rock to find his own.

Rhuaridh caught the brief nod from Des. They'd been at school together years ago. He moved closer to the boy. 'Kai? How are you? I heard you jumped off the waterfall.'

His eyes were scanning up and down Kai's body. There was an angry-looking projection underneath the wetsuit covering his left foreleg.

He touched Kai's shoulders. 'One of your

friends said you couldn't feel your legs, is that still true?'

'I wish!' said Kai loudly as he groaned again.

Des caught Rhuaridh's eye. 'He said at the beginning he couldn't feel his legs but that was literally only for a few moments. He's been feeling pain in his leg ever since, and for obvious reasons I've not moved him.'

Rhuaridh nodded. He knew exactly what he'd find if he cut Kai's wetsuit open. The only question was whether the bone was protruding from the skin. Right now, it was covered by the wetsuit and still protected.

Rhuaridh turned around and tugged the portable stretcher free from its packaging and started opening it out. There was no way Kai would be able to walk or swim anywhere.

Des had worked as an instructor at the wilderness centre for years and was experienced enough to need little direction. He helped unfold the stretcher while Rhuaridh took some time to assess Kai. He held his hands above the injured leg. 'Okay, I promise I'm not going to touch that bit. But I am going to take a look.' He pulled a torch from his backpack and checked the skin colour. 'Can you wiggle your toes?'

Kai grimaced but wiggled his toes while letting out a low yelp.

'Allergic to anything?'

Kai shook his head.

'How old are you?'

'Fourteen.'

'Any medical conditions I should know about? Or any regular medicines you need to take?'

Kai shook his head to both questions.

'Do you know how much you weigh?'

'Why?'

'I'm going to give you something to ease the pain. We're going to have to help you onto the stretcher, then carry you out through the waterfall. There's no other way out of here.'

Kai shook his head. 'No way. I can't stand the water pounding on my leg.'

Rhuaridh pulled out some kit. 'There's a metal hoop that fits on top of the stretcher. This plastic can go over the top of the hoop. It will keep the water off your leg, and hopefully protect you.' He looked at the water cascading past his shoulder. 'There *is* no other way out of here. We can get you in the stretcher, but we couldn't manoeuvre it upright to slide you through the space at the side.'

He shook his head as he looked at it. 'I had to imitate a spider to get in here, and I still got soaked by the waterfall on the way in.' He turned to Des. 'You've been around here just as long as me. Can you think of any other way to get him out?'

Des shook his head too. 'Not a chance. He's almost the same size as you and me. There's no way we could manoeuvre him. We just need to go straight through the waterfall.'

Rhuaridh calculated how much pain relief to give Kai and administered it quickly. 'We'll give it some time to take effect before we get you onto the stretcher.'

The radio at his waist crackled. 'Rhuaridh? Rhuaridh, are you there?'

Kristie's voice echoed around the cave. 'Who's that?' asked Des.

Rhuaridh pulled the radio from his waistband. 'What's up, Kristie?'

'They're not here yet and he's starting to wake up.'

'The ambulance crew haven't arrived?' He

was surprised. He'd expected them to arrive a few minutes after he left.

'No.' Her voice sounded kind of strained. 'Gerry's here. He got dropped back at our car and came himself. Apparently the ambulance had to stop at a road accident. They've taken the people to the hospital.'

Rhuaridh shook his head. Typical. Everything happened at once. The ambulance hadn't been used at all in the last week and now two simultaneous calls.

'Kristie, tell me the numbers on the monitor.'

There was silence for a few seconds, then her voice came through. 'The P is eighty-six. That's his pulse, isn't it?'

'That's fine. What's the other one?'

'It's ninety-seven.'

'That's his oxygen saturation. That's good. It means his breathing and lungs are okay.'

'Uh-oh.'

Rhuaridh sat up on his knees. 'What do you mean, "uh-oh"? Kristie?'

There was a crackle. Then a rumble of voices—all muffled. It was hard to hear anything with the constant background roar of falling water. Rhuaridh exchanged a look with

Des. He'd never met the other instructor at the centre. Throughout the year many instructors from different countries came to help at the centre—Des was the only real constant. 'Your guy. Anything I should know about him?'

Des's brow wrinkled. 'Ross?' He shook his head. 'Don't think so. He's been here about three weeks. Worked in a similar place in Wales.'

'Any medical history?'

Des pulled a face. 'To be honest, I can't remember. But if there had been anything major it would be on his initial application form.'

Rhuaridh knew that all the paperwork for the centre would be up to date. Des's wife dealt with that. But he also knew that Des wouldn't recall a single thing about it. He'd never been a paper person.

'Rhuaridh!' The shout came through the crackling radio and made all three in the cave start.

'Kristie, what's wrong?'

Even though it was difficult, he was on his feet, crouching in the cave. Staring at the rushing water that was currently between Kristie and himself.

'He's thrashing about. I think he's having some kind of seizure, what do I do?'

He could hear the panic in her voice. He signalled with his head to Des, who immediately pulled the prepared stretcher alongside Kai, knowing they would have to get out of there quickly.

'Do you know the recovery position?' he radioed to Kristie.

'W-hat?'

'His side. Turn him on his left-hand side. Get Gerry or some of the older kids to help you if need be. Once he's on his side pull up his right leg slightly and bring his right arm over so his hand is on the ground in front of him.'

And then there was nothing. No reply. No chatter. Just silence as his stomach churned. Either Ross's head injury had caused agitation and Kristie was mistaken, or he was having a full-blown seizure—neither of which were good signs. Kai would already need to be sent to the mainland for surgery. Now it looked like Ross would need to be airlifted. The nearest head injury unit was in Glasgow—it would take too long to get there by ambulance and ferry.

'Ready, Doc?'

Des had moved to Kai's head and shoulders, ready to slide the lad onto the stretcher. Rhua- ridh bent down straight away. 'Sure. Kai, your painkiller should have started working by now. We're going to slide you over onto the stretcher. It should only be a bit uncomfortable, and once you're on the stretcher the metal hoop will mean that nothing will touch your leg.'

He was trying hard to stay very calm, all while his brain wondered how Kristie was doing. He'd left her out there. He knew she wasn't medically qualified at all, but he'd felt duty bound to come and assess his other pa- tient. Would he have left her out there if he'd known the ambulance would be so long?

His mouth was dry. He couldn't help but re- member that momentary glance in her eyes when she'd told him hospitals freaked her out. He'd wanted to ask more, but there hadn't been time. He was drawn to this woman. He liked her. He couldn't ignore the flicker of attraction that seemed to permeate the air around them. But the truth was he barely knew her.

He was moving on autopilot. 'Ready?' he asked Kai.

The teenage boy screwed up his face and Des

held him by the shoulders and Rhuaridh gently took the weight off his legs. The movement was swift, with only a minor yelp from Kai. Des helped move the plastic casing quickly over the stretcher, zipping it closed, protecting the rest of Kai's body and only leaving his face exposed.

'Who is going first?' Des asked as he eyed the cascading waterfall. Each of them was going to have to step through it carrying the stretcher.

'I'll do it,' said Rhuaridh quickly. He tried the radio again. 'Kristie, how are you? How is Ross? Have you got him in the recovery position?'

There was an agonising pause.

'I think so. But he's still…twitching.'

'I'll be right there.' He could hear the tension in her voice. He wanted to jump straight through the waterfall and be by her side. But he was a doctor. He was so used to taking the emotion out of things and doing the duty he was bound to—like now, when he had to try and take care of two injured patients. Where was that darned ambulance?

Before he had chance to let his brain churn

any more he signalled to Kai and Des. 'Are we ready?'

They nodded. Rhuaridh looked at Kai. 'When I give you the signal, take a deep breath. I'll have the front end of the stretcher and we'll literally just need to walk through the waterfall. You know the pond isn't particularly deep. This isn't dangerous. Just a few moments of pounding water around your ears.'

Kai nodded. 'I've been through it once when Des pulled me back in here. I'll be okay. Let's get this over with.'

Rhuaridh put the rest of the equipment back in the rucksack and put it on his back. He jumped down into the pool with the waterfall directly at his back. The noise was deafening, so he used signals to grab the stretcher above his shoulders and gesture to Kai. Des was ready and they moved swiftly through the waterfall and back out into the pool. Water cascaded over them, but it only took a few seconds to be free of the noise and clear their noses and mouths.

From the crest of the hill he could see a flash of bright green. The paramedics had finally arrived. Most of the kids were still crowded around the sides of the pool. They waded slowly across, setting Kai down gently as his friends surrounded him. One of the paramedics knelt beside him, and the other joined Rhuaridh at Kristie's side.

Her eyes were glinting with fear. 'He's literally just stopped shaking. He seemed to wake up for a few seconds, thrashing his legs and arms out, then he started shaking again.'

There was a red mark on the side of her cheek.

'Did you get caught by his arm?' asked Rhuaridh.

She shook her head. 'I'm fine. It doesn't matter.'

But it did to Rhuaridh.

It only took a few moments to assess Ross and to arrange an air ambulance for him. His pupil reactions were sluggish now and it was obvious the knock to the head had been harsh. He needed proper assessment in a specialist centre.

Rhuaridh then took time to recheck Kai before loading him up in the ambulance with the paramedics, ready for transfer for surgery.

By the time the ambulance had left with both patients, Des had gathered the teenagers together to take them back to the wilderness centre. Gerry was still chatting to a few that he'd caught on film.

Kristie was standing at the side, dirt smudged on her cheek and on the knees of her trousers. Rhuaridh reached out, took her hand and led her off to the side, pulling her down next to him on a large overturned tree trunk that had fallen over years before.

'Are you okay? I'm sorry that I left you.'

She gave a small shake of her head, fixing her gaze on the view ahead.

He hadn't let go of her, enclosing one of her slim hands in both of his. She moved her gaze to meet his.

He held his breath. He couldn't help it. All he could focus on was the blue of her eyes. The hand he held between his was trembling slightly and he gave it a squeeze. 'I didn't mean to leave you alone so long. I thought the ambulance would only be a few minutes.'

Her voice was quiet. 'You had to go and check on the boy. I know that.' She gave a weak smile, 'You're a doctor. It's your job.'

'But it's not yours,' he replied, his voice hoarse.

She'd been shaking. She was pale. Pieces

were falling into place. Now he understood why she'd seemed distracted in the hospital. He'd thought she either wasn't that interested or had just had her mind on other things.

She'd been nervous. She'd been scared. And he'd missed it.

'Why don't you tell me why you don't like hospitals, Kristie?'

She licked her lips and shook her head. 'It's not something we need to talk about.'

She looked him straight in the eye and pulled her hand free from his, lifting it to touch his cheek. 'You just scaled part of a rock face and walked through a waterfall, Dr Gillespie. Some people might call that superhero material.'

'What would you call it?' The words were out instantly. Instinct. His gut reaction to that question. Because he really wanted to know the answer. He wanted to know exactly what Kristie Nelson thought about him.

If he'd thought for a few more seconds he'd have realised she'd just avoided his question. The one that might get to the heart of who she was.

'I haven't quite decided yet,' she whispered,

the edges of her mouth turning upwards. 'But things are looking up.'

Her hand on his skin was making his pulse race. His eyes went instinctively to her mouth. The mouth he wanted to kiss.

He moved forward, all rational thoughts leaving his brain as his lips firmly connected with hers. She reacted instantly, leaning in towards him and sliding one hand up the side of his neck. He knew she needed comfort. He knew she needed reassurance. This seemed so obvious, so natural and it looked like Kristie thought so too.

Her skin was cold, but her lips were warm. Sweet. Responsive. She didn't seem to mind they were sitting on a log in the middle of the damp countryside. She didn't seem to mind at all, and as her hand raked through his hair he could almost feel the temperature rising around them.

But little alarms were going off in his brain, like red flags frantically waving. How could he kiss her when he knew there was something else affecting her?

He took a deep breath. He reluctantly pulled back. For a moment, neither of them spoke—

just stared at each other as if they couldn't quite believe what had just happened.

Rhuaridh pressed his lips together for a second, doing his best to collect his thoughts. The ones he was currently having involved sweeping Kristie up into his arms, into his car and away from this whole place. But she'd said something. She'd revealed a part of herself that she hadn't before and every instinct told him that he had to try and peel back more of Kristie's layers.

'Wow,' she said softly as a hint of a smile touched her lips.

'Wow,' he agreed. His timing was all wrong. He looked at her steadily, keeping his voice even. 'Kristie, I do think we need to talk.'

There was a flash of momentary confusion in her eyes. He could almost see the shutters going down again, as if she knew what was about to come next.

He kept going. 'I think the reason you don't like hospitals is important. I think, when I work with someone, if something significant has happened in the past that affects how they feel or think about something, I should know.

I should know not to expose them to a situation that they might find hard.'

She pulled her hand back as if she'd been stung. 'Is that what we're doing, working together?'

It was the way she asked the question—as if those words actually hurt—that made him catch his breath. He could hear it in her voice. The unspoken question. Was that all it was? Particularly after that kiss…

But she didn't wait for an answer. She just brushed off her trousers, stood up and walked away…for the second time.

CHAPTER SIX

October

SHE CLOSED HER social media account. *Will they? Won't they?* seemed to be everywhere she looked. She'd even been invited on a talk show to discuss her blossoming 'relationship' with Rhuaridh Gillespie, the world's hottest Highland doc.

'I'm going to kill you, Gerry,' she muttered.

He was staring out of the ferry window at the thrashing sea, rubbing his chest distractedly. 'No, you're not. You've got the most popular show on the network. You love it.'

'I don't have time to love it. I can't get a minute of peace.' She rubbed her eyes and leaned against the wall.

'What's wrong?' he asked.

She sighed. 'There was a call last night.' She rubbed her hands up both arms. It was cold. Scotland was much colder than LA, but that chill had seemed to come out of nowhere. 'It was hard. I don't know if I helped. I've spent the whole journey wondering if...' Her voice trailed off.

Gerry touched her shoulder. 'Don't. You volunteer. You counsel. You're the person who listens in the middle of the night when someone needs to talk. You do the best that you can. That's all you can do.'

She put her head back on the wall. Fatigue sweeping over her. 'I know that. But I can't help but worry.'

'You don't look that great,' said Gerry.

She closed her eyes for a second. 'I don't feel that great. I forgot to take my seasickness tablets. I'll be fine when we land.'

The truth was she was nervous, and a little bit sad. She wasn't quite sure what to say to Rhuaridh. She'd felt the connection. And she was sure he had too.

Didn't their kiss prove it? But that had been fleeting. Rhuaridh had stopped it almost as soon as it had started. And then he'd pressed about the thing she didn't want to talk about. Wasn't ready to talk about.

And it had haunted her for the last month. Her

head even felt fuzzy right now. She loosened the scarf she'd wound around her neck. It was irritating her. They'd started filming earlier, following up on Ross, the instructor with the head injury last month, who'd had emergency surgery. He was staying in Glasgow, recovering well, even though he was pale with a large part of his hair now missing. The young boy, Kai, had his leg in a cast but took great delight in showing them just how fast he could get about on his crutches.

Thank goodness those two parts of filming were wrapped up. It would mean they would need less footage whilst on Arran. She closed her eyes, part of her not wanting to spend too much time in Rhuaridh's company and part of her aching for it.

She was so confused right now. And who was making all that noise? She shivered, pulling her coat closer around her. Rhuaridh. Sometimes thinking about him made her angry, sometimes it made her feel warm all over. Her mind would drift back to that second on the beach…then that second sitting in the woods together. Her life currently felt like a bad young adult romance novel.

'Kristie. Kristie.' Someone was shaking her. 'We need to go. Here, give me the keys. I'll drive.'

'What? No?' She stood up and promptly swayed and sat back down. Had she actually fallen asleep?

Gerry was looking at her oddly. 'You're sick,' he said, holding out his hand for the car key. 'I'll drive. It's the same place as last time.'

She thought about saying no. She knew Gerry didn't like driving 'abroad', as he put it. But she was just so darned tired. She pushed the keys towards him. 'Okay, just once. And don't crash.'

'Kristie? You need to drink something.'

She moved, wondering why the bed felt so lumpy, trying to turn around, but her face met an unexpected barrier. She spluttered and opened her eyes. Dark blue was facing her. What?

She pushed herself back, trying to work out why there was a solid wall of dark blue in the bedroom in the cottage.

The voice started again. 'Kristie? Turn back this way. You need to drink something.'

Her brain wasn't making sense. Was she dreaming?

She moved back around again. Opening her eyes properly. They took a moment to focus. Directly ahead was a flickering orange fire. She pushed herself up, the material underneath her unfamiliar, velvety to touch. She looked down. She wasn't in her bed in the cottage. In fact, she didn't recognise this place at all. 'What? Wh…where am I?'

A face appeared before her. One she couldn't mistake.

'Rhuaridh?'

He nodded and knelt at the side of what she presumed must be his sofa. 'Here.' He held a glass of water with a straw. 'Will you drink something?'

Her throat felt dry and scratchy. She grabbed the straw and took a drink of the cold water. Nothing had ever tasted so good.

She moved, swinging her legs so she was sitting up right. 'Ooh…' Her head felt as if she'd been pushed from side to side.

'Careful. You haven't sat up for over a day.'

She blinked and took a few breaths, looking down at the large, soft white T-shirt she was wearing, along with an unfamiliar pair of grey brushed-cotton pyjama bottoms.

'Whose are these? And...' she looked about again '...how did I end up here?'

Rhuaridh pulled a face. 'The clothes? I guess they're yours. I had to buy emergency supplies for you. And you ended up here because Gerry panicked. He couldn't wake you up or get you out the car after you landed from the ferry. Your temperature was through the roof and you were quite confused.'

'I was?' She hated that she couldn't remember a single thing about this. 'But...you're busy. You don't have time to look after someone.' She was suddenly very self-conscious that she staying in the doctor's house.

He shrugged. 'I'm the doctor. It's what I do.'

Her head was feeling a little straighter. She tugged at the T-shirt self-consciously. 'What's been wrong with me?'

'You've had some kind of virus.'

'You're a doctor, and that's all you can tell me?' she asked, without trying to hide her surprise.

'Yes,' he said as he smiled. 'Your temperature has gone up and down as your body has fought off the virus. It made you a bit confused at times. You needed sleep to give your body a chance to do the work it had to.'

'Why didn't you send me to hospital?'

'Because you didn't need to go to hospital. You needed complete rest, simple paracetamol and some fluids.' He stood up. 'And some chicken soup—which I've just finished making. I'll go and get you some.'

He walked away towards the kitchen then ducked back and gave her a cheeky wink. 'You gave me five minutes of panic, though—you had a bit of a rash.'

She stared down in horror, wondering where on earth the rash had been—and how he had seen it.

All of a sudden she realised that someone had changed her into these clothes and put her others somewhere else. She looked around the room. It was larger than she might have expected. Comfortably decorated with a wooden coffee table between her and the flickering fire, the large navy-blue sofa and armchairs. At the far end of the room next to one of the windows was a dining table and chairs, with some bookshelves built into the walls. Part of her wanted to sneak over and check his reading materials.

Rhuaridh appeared a few moments later carrying a tray. The smell of the soup alone made her stomach growl. He laughed as he sat down next to her, his leg brushing against hers.

He slid the tray over towards her. There was a pot of tea, a bowl of chicken and rice soup that looked so thick she could stand her spoon in it, and some crusty bread and butter.

'Aren't you having some?' she asked, conscious of the fact she'd be eating in front of him. He nodded. 'Give me a sec.' He walked back through to the kitchen then joined her on the sofa as she took her first spoonful of soup.

It was delicious. Not like anything they had in LA. Soup wasn't that popular there. But she'd noticed in Scotland a whole variety of soups seemed a staple part of the diet. 'You actually made this?'

He nodded. 'From an old recipe of my dad's. I can make this one, Scotch broth, lentil and bacon, and tomato.' He frowned as he was thinking. 'I can also make mince and potatoes, stovies, steak pie, and chicken and leek pie. After that? My menu kind of falls off a cliff.'

'Okay, is this where I admit I only know what part of that menu is?'

She was starting to feel a little more alive. Now she'd woken up and orientated herself, she wasn't quite so embarrassed by what had happened. Rhuaridh had looked after a million patients. He was a doctor. It was his job.

She kept on spooning up the soup. 'I think this is the best thing I've ever tasted,' she admitted. 'You'll need to teach me. I can't make anything like this. In fact, avocado and toast is about my limit.'

'What do you eat in LA?'

She grinned. 'Avocado and toast. And anything else that I buy in a store.'

She liked the way he laughed. Deep and hearty.

It didn't take long to finish the soup. She sighed and leaned back on the sofa. 'That was great.'

His hand brushed against hers as he moved the tea on the table in front of her and lifted her soup bowl. It made her start.

'I wonder… I know it's been an imposition having me here, but could I use your shower before I get ready to go back to my own cottage?'

He pointed to the staircase. 'There's a spare room with an en suite bathroom at the top of the stairs. Some of your things are in there. I only brought you down here when you were so cold—so the fire could heat you.'

He'd carried her. He'd carried her down here. The intimacy of the act made her cheeks blaze unexpectedly.

As Rhuaridh made his way back to the kitchen, she practically ran up the stairs. Sure enough, the white bedclothes were rumpled and there was a bag with her clothes at the side. Her stomach flip-flopped. She grabbed what she could and headed to the shower.

He'd spent the last day worrying about her. When Gerry had turned up at his door, it had taken him all his time to assess her to reassure himself that there was nothing serious going on.

The sigh that Gerry had finally let out when Rhuaridh had told him that it was likely she had some kind of virus her body was fighting off had filled the room. He'd sent Gerry back to the rental, advising him that he'd watch over her.

Against his spare white bedding she'd looked pale, her normal tan bleached from her skin, and her temperature had been raging. He'd had to strip her clothes off, then try and dose her with some paracetamol whilst she'd been barely conscious.

He'd known it would pass. He'd known it was part and parcel of the body fighting off a virus—and sleeping was the best thing she could do. But it didn't stop him settling into a chair in the corner of the room and spending an uncomfortable night there, watching over Kristie.

Next day he'd run out to the nearest shop to buy her something to wear as the virus ran its course and she went from hot to cold. He'd had a heart-stopping minute when he'd pulled back the bedclothes and seen the red rash all over her abdomen. But it had faded just as quickly as it had appeared and he'd pulled the pyjamas onto her.

Now she was awake and showering—and would probably want to leave. And he was struck by how sorry he was about that. He'd never shared this cottage with anyone. Since he'd moved to Arran he hadn't brought anyone back to this space. Mac was watching carefully from the corner. He'd come over and sniffed at Kristie a few times, then nudged her in the hope she'd wake up and bring him food. When that hadn't happened he'd slumped off to the corner again.

It had been over a year since Rhuaridh had lived with someone. The penthouse flat that he'd shared with Zoe in one of the central areas of Glasgow didn't have the charm of this old cottage. Its plain white walls and sterile glass now seemed to Rhuaridh like some kind of indicator of their relationship. Zoe had liked living with a colleague who was doing well. Someone she thought might 'go places'. Of course, that had all come to a resounding crash when he'd told her his intention to return home to Arran as a general practitioner.

He couldn't remember the strength of his feelings back then. If Zoe had been sick, would she even have wanted Rhuaridh to take care of her—the way he had Kristie? It was likely not. There were no similarities between the two women. Zoe didn't have the warmth that Kristie did. Even when Kristie was sick, she'd still occasionally reached out and squeezed his hand.

There was something about that connection. That taking care of someone. Letting them share the space that was essentially yours. Somehow with Kristie it didn't feel intrusive. It just felt…right. He'd never experienced that with Zoe. Instead, he'd just felt like part of her grand plan. One that had come to a resounding halt when he'd said he was moving back to Arran. Rejection always hurt. That, and the feeling of not being 'enough' for someone. He had none of that from Kristie. Instead, it felt like they were pieces of the same puzzle— albeit from thousands of miles apart—that just seemed to fit together. And it didn't matter that long term it all seemed impossible, because right now was all he wanted to think about.

Rhuaridh turned as Kristie came back down the stairs. Her damp hair was tied up, her cheeks looked a bit pinker and she'd changed into the clothes that Gerry had stuck in a bag and brought around yesterday. 'Stole some of your deodorant,' she said apologetically. 'Gerry's idea of toiletries seems to be only a toothbrush.'

'No worries,' he said casually. He pointed to the table. 'I made some more tea. I thought you wouldn't be ready for anything more sociable.'

She eyed the tea and accompanying plate of chocolate biscuits. 'That's about as sociable as I can manage,' she said as she sat back on the sofa and tucked her legs underneath her. 'Hey, Mac,' she said, calling the dog over and rubbing his head, 'I'm sorry, have I been ignoring you?' She bent down and dropped a kiss on his head. 'Promise you it wasn't intentional.'

She let Rhuaridh pour the tea and hand her a cup before he sat down next to her again. The pink T-shirt she was wearing made her look more like herself.

'I'm glad you're feeling better,' he said. And he meant it.

She sipped her tea. 'I'm so sorry. I've really put you out. What about work?'

He looked at her and gave a gentle shake of his head. 'It's Sunday. You arrived late on Friday night and there's been a locum on call at the hospital this weekend.'

Her eyes widened as she realised what those words meant. Her hand flew to her mouth.

'Your first weekend off? Oh, no. I'm so sorry. You must have had plans.'

He shrugged. 'I guess you changed them for me.'

She blinked. Her eyes looked wet. 'I'm sorry,' she whispered, her voice a bit croaky.

'Don't be. You brightened up our weekend. Mac's getting bored with me anyhow. He likes the change of company.'

She gave him a curious glance. 'Do you normally bring patients back to your house?'

He paused, knowing exactly how this would sound. 'There's a first time for everything.'

Her breathing faltered and that made his own hitch. He wondered if she'd say something else but instead she sighed and leaned back against the sofa again. 'We've missed filming. We won't have time to get much more.'

'Gerry didn't seem too worried. To be honest, after his initial moment of panic, he almost seemed relieved. I think the guy might need a bit of a break.'

'You've spoken to Gerry?'

'He's been round a few times.' He didn't add that Gerry might have filmed her while she'd slept. That was for Gerry to sort out. According to Gerry, a host's consent was implicit, it was built into their contract—no matter what the situation.

She shuffled a little on the sofa and rested her head on his shoulder. 'We got some footage before we got here. You know about Kai and Ross?'

He was surprised. He hadn't realised they were being so thorough. 'I knew that you followed up on Magda and the baby, but I didn't know you'd followed up on all the other patients too.'

She lifted her head and looked him in the eye. 'Of course. The viewers love it. They want to know if everyone is okay. Haven't you realised that human beings are essentially nosy creatures and want to know everything?'

He could answer that question in so many ways. He could laugh. He could crack a joke. But he didn't.

He'd looked after Kristie for the last twenty-four hours. And at so many points in that time he'd wished he didn't only get to spend three days at a time with her. He'd wished all their time wasn't spent filming. He'd prefer it if it could just be them, without anyone else, no patients, no cameras.

So he didn't make a joke because this was it. This was the time to ask the question he should have asked before.

'Why don't you tell me?' he said gently.

'Tell me what?'

'Tell me why you don't like hospitals.' He could see it instantly. The shadow passing over her eyes.

She swallowed and stared into the fire for a few moments, then reached up and brushed her hand against her damp hair. She wasn't looking at him. He could see he'd lost her to some past memory. Maybe it was the only way she could do this.

'I don't like hospitals because I had to go there...' her voice trembled '...when my sister died.'

The words cut into him like a knife. Now he understood. Now he knew why he could always tell that something was amiss.

'It's everything,' she continued. 'The lights, the smell, the busyness, and even the quiet. The overall sound and bustle of the place.' Now she turned to meet his gaze and he could see just how exposed she was. 'And it doesn't matter where in the world the hospital is because, essentially, they're all the same. And they all evoke the same memories for me.'

He was nodding now as he reached out and took one of her hands in his, intertwining their fingers. 'This job?' she said, as she dipped her head. 'It was the absolute last one that I wanted. I wanted the Egyptian museum. I wanted the astronaut's life. Not because I thought they were more exciting, just because I knew they wouldn't bring me to a hospital. And you—' she looked straight at him '—were always going to do that to me.'

He kept nodding. He was beginning to understand her a little more. Just like he wanted to. But she hadn't answered the most important question. 'What happened to your sister, Kristie?'

She blinked, her eyes filled with tears. 'I don't talk about it,' she whispered. 'Hardly anyone knows.'

'You don't have to tell me. I want you to trust me, Kristie. I want you to know that I'm your friend.' Friend? Was that what you called someone he'd kissed the way he'd kissed her?

He was treading carefully. He had to. He could tell how delicate this all was for her. Holding hands was as much as she could handle right now and he knew that.

She closed her eyes and kept them that way. 'My sister was unwell. She'd been unwell for a long time, and…' a tear slid down her cheek '…felt that no one was listening. She took her own life.'

The words finished with a sob and he pulled her forward into his arms.

He didn't speak. He knew there was nothing he could say right now that would help. She'd told him hardly anyone knew and she didn't really talk about it, so this had been building up in her for a long time. Pain didn't lessen with time, often it was amplified. Often it became even more raw than it had been before.

He hated Kristie feeling that way, so he stayed there and he held her, stroking her hair and her back softly until she was finally all cried out.

'I'm sorry,' he whispered.

She lifted her head and tilted her face towards his. 'You said we were friends,' she said hoarsely. 'Are we friends? Because what I'm feeling… I don't feel that way about a friend.'

He could feel his heart thudding in his chest. It was almost as if she'd been reading his mind for the past two months—ever since they'd sat on that log together. Since they'd shared that kiss. 'How do you feel?'

She reached up and touched the side of his face. 'How many people have you looked after in your house?' she asked.

'None.'

'How many people have you made chicken soup for?' She tilted her head and smiled at him.

He couldn't help but return that smile. 'None.'

She slid her hand up around his neck. 'Then I'm going to take it for granted that all of this...' she paused '...means something.'

'I think you could be right,' he whispered as he bent forward and finally put his lips on hers.

And all of sudden everything felt right.

CHAPTER SEVEN

November

'I'M SORRY, MISS. That's the just the way is it. We've cancelled the ferries for the rest of today. We can't take them out in a storm like this. We'd never get docked on the other side, it's not safe for the passengers or the crew.'

She could feel panic start to creep up her chest.

'But you'll sail tomorrow, won't you?'

He shook his head. 'Not likely. The storm's forecast to be even worse tomorrow. And it's to last the next day too. It could be Thursday before the ferries are sailing again.'

She couldn't breathe. She couldn't miss filming—not because of the show but because, if she didn't film, she didn't get to spend time with Rhuaridh. The guy she'd been counting down the last four weeks for. The guy she'd been texting every day. And most nights.

Gerry shook his head. 'Louie won't be happy with this. We'll need to use whatever unused footage we have.' He made a bit of a face and walked away.

The man at the ferry terminal gave her a shrug. 'Sorry, it only usually happens around twice a year. Storms get so bad no one can get off or on the island.'

'But there must be another way? A smaller boat? A helicopter? What if there's a medical emergency?'

The man gave her a look. 'To take a smaller boat out in this weather would be suicide. As for emergencies, everyone on the island knows that this can sometimes happen. If the doc can't fix it, it can't be fixed.'

She stepped back. He'd got her with that word. *Suicide*. She'd been desperate. She'd been ready to run around the harbour to try and charter a smaller boat. But she wouldn't do that now. Not after that word.

She looked out through the glass at the ferry terminal. She couldn't even see Arran on the horizon, just the mass of grey swirling storm, and hear the thud of the pouring rain.

Another month without seeing Rhuaridh again?

It had never seemed so long.

CHAPTER EIGHT

December

HE WAS WAITING at the ferry terminal. It was ridiculous. She would be driving the hire car but he still wanted to see her. Two months. Two months since their second kiss.

Sometimes he felt guilty, thinking he'd taken advantage. But from the stream of messages they'd exchanged since then, there had been no indication that she thought that.

Was it possible to actually get to know some-one better by text, email and a few random video chats? Because it felt like it was. He'd learned that Kristie's favourite position was sitting on her chair at home, in her yoga pants, eating raisins.

She'd learned that he was addicted to an orange-coloured now sugar-free fizzy drink that some people called Scotland's national drink. He didn't let many people know that. She'd also laughed as she'd watched him try to follow a new recipe and increase his limited kitchen menu, and fail dismally.

It was only when he was standing on the snow-covered dock that he realised he'd no idea what car she would be driving this time. But she spotted him first, flashing her head-lights and pulling to a stop next to him in the car park.

'Hey!' She jumped out of the car with a wide smile on her face. At first she looked as if she was about to throw her arms around him, but something obviously stopped her as she halted midway and looked a bit awkward. Instead, she held out her hands. 'Snow,' she said simply as she looked about.

She lifted her chin up towards the gently fall-ing snow, closing her eyes and smiling as she spun around.

Gerry got out of the car and looked mildly amused.

'You've never seen snow before?' asked Rhuaridh.

'Of course I haven't,' she said, still spinning around. 'I live in LA. It's hardly snow central.'

Rhuaridh looked over at Gerry. 'What about you?'

Gerry shook his head. 'Don't worry about me. I spent three months filming in Alaska. I *know* snow.'

Rhuaridh smiled as he kept watching Kristie. He'd never realised this would be her first experience of snow. 'It's not even lying properly,' he said. 'Give it another day and we might actually be able to build a snowman or have a snowball fight.'

'Really?' She stopped spinning, her eyes sparkling.

He nodded. 'Sure. Now come on, I'm taking you two guys to dinner in the pub just down the road. Let's go.'

'Good for me,' said Gerry quickly, climbing back into the car.

Kristie stepped up in front of him. 'You don't have to do that,' she said, still smiling.

She was so close he caught the scent of her perfume. It was different, something headier. 'But I want to.' He slid his hand behind her, holding her for the briefest of seconds. 'I might have missed having you around.'

'Good.' She blinked as a large snowflake landed on her eyelashes. 'Let's keep that up.'

Part of her was excited and part of her was laced with a tiny bit of trepidation. Louie was massively excited. It seemed he'd taken over production of the episode where she'd been unwell and had included footage of Rhuaridh looking after her, interspersed with a few repetitions of their previous interactions.

It wasn't her favourite episode because it felt so intrusive. The whole episode was literally dedicated to the relationship between them, rather than the life of a Highland doc. But Louie had argued his case well. 'The viewers have been waiting for this. They want it. And what else have we got to show them this month? You didn't exactly do any filming on the island, we were lucky Gerry actually filmed anything at all.'

She knew in a way he was right. But when she'd taken on this role, she hadn't realised the story would become about her too.

Watching the scenes where Rhuaridh had

been looking after her had brought a lump to her throat. He was so caring. So quietly concerned. It was a side of him she hadn't seen before. And the way that he'd looked at her at times had made her heart melt. Thank goodness Gerry hadn't been around to film their kiss. She hadn't told him about either of the times they'd kissed. He was already looking at her a bit suspiciously—as if he suspected something—so she didn't plan on revealing anything more.

The pub that Rhuaridh took them to was warm and welcoming, panelled with wood. Every table was taken and the pub was full of Christmas decorations—twinkling lights, a large decorated tree and red and green garlands underneath the bar. Rhuaridh insisted they all eat a traditional Scottish Christmas dinner—turkey, stuffing, roast potatoes, tiny sausages, Brussels sprouts and mashed turnip all covered in gravy. 'This is delicious,' said Gerry. 'A bit more like our Thanksgiving dinner. But I like it. I could eat more of this.'

Kristie leaned back and rubbed her stomach, groaning. 'No way. I couldn't eat another single thing.'

Rhuaridh was watching them both with a smile on his face. 'Well, I'm still trying to make up for the fact you spent a few days here eating hardly anything.'

'Are you trying to take care of me, Dr Gillespie?' she teased.

He shook his head. 'No way. You're far too difficult a patient.' There was a twinkle in his eyes as he said the word. He glanced at Gerry, obviously not wanting this conversation to become too personal. 'What are your plans for filming this time? Do we need to make up for lost time?'

Kristie shifted a little uncomfortably, not quite sure how to tell him about the episode that would go out in a few weeks, but Gerry got in there first. 'Don't worry,' he said with a wave of his hand, 'we've got that covered. We had some old unused footage and just mixed it with the fact that Kristie was pretty much out of action.'

'Oh, okay.' Rhuaridh seemed to accept the explanation easily. 'So what about this time?'

Kristie had given this some thought. 'We've got quite a bit of footage of some of the patients in the cottage hospital. Christmas is a big deal. I know we're not actually here for Christmas Day, but it might be nice if we could get some film of how the staff deal with patients who they know will have to stay in hospital for Christmas.'

Rhuaridh lifted his eyebrows. 'You mean, you actually want some heart-warming stuff for Christmas instead of some kind of crisis?'

Gerry laughed. 'If you can whip us up a crisis we'll always take it, but I think we were going to try and keep with the season of goodwill. On a temporary basis, of course.'

Rhuaridh looked carefully at Kristie. 'Do you feel okay about filming in the hospital?'

Gerry's eyebrows shot upwards. He had no idea that she'd shared her secret with the doc. Kristie cleared her throat awkwardly, trying to buy a bit of time. But she could come up with nothing. It seemed that honesty might be for the best.

'He knows about Jess. I told him.'

She couldn't decipher the look Gerry gave her. 'Okay, then,' he said simply.

She took a few moments. She'd thought about this when Louie had suggested it. Everything previously had seemed like a diktat—it had

been required for the show so she'd had to
grit her teeth and get on with it. She'd been so
fixated on how she felt about hospitals, deep
down, that she hadn't taken the time to recon-
sider how her perspective might have changed
a little. 'We're talking about the older patients
who are too sick to get home. You know I met
some of them before?'

Rhuaridh nodded.

She smiled as things seemed to click in her
mind. 'I actually really enjoyed talking with
some of them. They're not patients. They're
people. People who've lived long, very interesting lives and have a hundred tales to tell.
Maybe we should try and film an update on a
few of the people we've spoken to before—and
maybe we should ask them about Christmases
from years gone by. How did people normally
celebrate Christmas on Arran? Are there any
special traditions?'

Rhuaridh and Gerry exchanged a glance and
looked at her, then at each other again.

Gerry leaned over the table. 'What do you
think's happened to her?'

'I think she's turned into some kind of
Christmas holiday movie. You know—the

kind that play on that TV channel constantly at Christmas.'

Kristie laughed and nudged both of them. 'Stop it, you guys. Maybe I'm just getting into the spirit of things. First time I've seen snow. First time I've been in a place that's cold at Christmas. All my life I've spent my Christmases in sunshine next to a pool. Give a girl a break. I'm just getting in the mood.'

As soon as she said the words she felt her cheeks flush. She hadn't quite meant it to come out like that. Gerry didn't seem to notice, but she knew that Rhuaridh did as he gave her a gentle nudge with his leg under the table.

'It's settled, then,' said Gerry as he raised his pint glass towards them. 'Tomorrow we go be festive!'

Arran in the snow was truly gorgeous. He hadn't paid much attention before because snow in winter was the norm here. But somehow, seeing it through Kristie's eyes gave him a whole new perspective on how much the whole island looked like a Christmas-card scene.

Now, as he looked out of the window as they pulled up at the hospital, he took a deep breath and let himself love everything that he could see. He always had loved this place, but the break-up with Zoe had left him living under an uncomfortable cloud. Her words had continued to echo in his head.

'It's an island in the middle of nowhere. There's not a single thing to do on that place. How anyone can stay there more than one night is beyond me. I'd be bored witless in the first week.'

Those words had continued to wear away at him. The place where he'd grown up and loved hadn't been good enough for the woman he'd loved at that time. *He* hadn't been good enough for her.

His loyalties had felt tested to their limit. The loyalties and love he had for the place he'd called home, and his loyalties to his profession, his future dreams, and the woman he'd lived with.

For the first time he actually realised what a blessing it had been that things had come to a head.

He'd always wondered if the move to Arran again was just a temporary move—to fill the gap until someone else could be recruited for the GP surgery. But in the last two months things had changed and he couldn't help but wonder if the TV show was the cause of that.

For the first time in for ever there had been applicants for the GP locum weekend cover posts that had been advertised for as long as Rhuaridh had been here. That was why he'd had cover the last time Kristie had been here. Other GPs were taking an interest in Arran. He'd had some random emails, one asking about covering Magda's maternity leave, and another from a doctor who wanted to complete his GP training on the island. That had never happened before.

Before, he'd felt he was stuck here.

Now he knew he was choosing to stay here. And that made all the difference.

Kristie had a piece of red tinsel in her hair. 'Are we going in, or are we sitting here?'

He smiled. 'Let's go. I'm going to review a few patients while we're here.'

Gerry tagged behind a little, almost like he was giving them a bit of space. Rhuaridh wondered just how much the cameraman suspected. He'd been so tempted to give Kristie a kiss when she'd first arrived that he wondered if Gerry had noticed that.

Rhuaridh watched as Kristie entered the hospital. Her footsteps faltered a little but she held her head up high and ran her hand along the wall as she entered the building. It was like she was using it to steady herself. He paused for a second, then stopped worrying about who was around and who would see.

She'd shared with him why she was antsy around hospitals. She'd shared a part of herself. He walked alongside her and took her other hand in his, giving it a squeeze. She looked down—surprised—then squeezed back. He didn't say anything. He didn't have to.

They carried on down the corridor.

They were only in the hospital for a few minutes before one of the nursing assistants grabbed Kristie and persuaded her to help put up some more decorations.

'We can't put them in the clinical areas, but we can put them at the entrance and in the patients' day room.'

'No tree on the ward?' he heard Kristie say. She looked quite sad.

Rhuaridh shook his head. 'Infection control issues. Also allergies—they harbour dust. Health and safety too—they could be a fire risk.'

'Phew.' Kristie let out a huge sigh. 'How do you remember so many interesting rules and regulations?' She rolled her eyes. 'And here was me thinking that Christmas decorations would have a place in hospitals—to improve mental health, lift spirits, and to help orientate some of the older patients to time and place.'

He raised his eyebrows. 'Touché. What have you been reading?'

'Lots.' She smiled. 'I'm not just a pretty face.' Her words hung there as they smiled at each other, then she glanced over her shoulder as the nursing assistant appeared with another box. 'Or just an objectionable reporter,' she added quickly.

He pointed to the half-erected tree. 'This has been here for as long as I have. And, Ms Objectionable Reporter, the stuff you say about lifting spirits and orientating to time and place is right. But...' he paused '...our biggest issue in this season is winter vomiting—also known as norovirus. If we end up with that?' He held up his hands and shook his head. 'There's a huge outbreak cleaning protocol, and something like this would have to be taken down and disposed of if it had been in a clinical area.' He gave a shrug. 'Better safe than sorry.'

She picked up a piece of sparkling green tinsel and draped it around his neck. 'Aw, it's a shame. Maybe you could impersonate the Christmas tree instead?'

'Ha-ha. Now, don't you have patients to film?'

'Don't you have patients to see?'

The nursing assistant's head turned from side to side, smiling at the flirtation and teasing going on before her very eyes. 'Glad to see you two are finally getting on,' she said under her breath.

It gave Rhuaridh a bit of a jolt and he nodded and strode towards the ward. 'Catch up if you can,' he shouted over his shoulder.

He spent the next hour reviewing patients, writing prescriptions and watching Kristie out of the corner of his eye. She seemed easier, relaxed even. By now everyone was used to Gerry hovering around in the background with the camera.

It was nice to see her that way. She had a long conversation with one of the older men who was recuperating after a hip operation. She tried a few Christmas carols with a couple of the female patients. She helped put out cups of tea and coffee, and was particularly interested in the range of cakes that appeared from the hospital kitchen.

'It's like a baker's shop,' she said in wonder.

The nurse near her nodded. 'We find that often appetites are smaller when patients get older. Our kitchen staff are great. The cook was even in earlier, asking people what their favourites were. That's why we have Bakewell tarts, Empire biscuits and fairy cakes.'

Rhuaridh heard Kristie whisper, 'Don't you get into trouble about the sugar?'

The nurse shook her head. 'Not at this point. Calories are important. Look around. Most of our patients are underweight, not overweight. We'd rather feed them what they like than look at artificial supplements.'

Kristie flitted from one patient to the next, squeezing hands and making jokes. Occasion-ally he glimpsed a far-off look in her eye that didn't last long. The patients loved her.

But the more he watched, the more he had nagging doubts. He couldn't pretend he didn't like her. The whole world could see that he did. But was the whole world also laughing at him? After all, what would a gorgeous girl from LA find interesting about a Scottish island? There were no TV studios, no job opportunities. Most of the time during winter half the island shut down. There was no cinema. No department stores—only a few local shops. There was one slightly posher hotel with a swimming pool, gym and spa but there wasn't a selection to choose from. And there were only two hair-dressers on the entire island. Kristie had already told him she loved trying different places.

Zoe's words echoed around his head. Boring. Dull. Nothing to do.

He hadn't been able to maintain a long-term relationship with a woman in Glasgow just over fifty miles away. How on earth could he even contemplate anything with a woman from LA—five thousand miles away? He must be losing his marbles.

Just at that moment, Kristie leaned forward and pressed her head against that of one of the older, more confused patients. He could see she was talking quietly to him. His hands were trembling, and Kristie put her own over his, squeezing them in reassurance. She pointed to the Christmas tree through the doors. She was orientating him to time and place.

And that was it. A little bit of his heart melted. Did it really matter if this would come to nothing? Maybe it was time for him to start living in the here and now.

And the here and now for him was that Kristie would still be visiting for three days a month for the next four months. And if that was all he'd get, he'd be a fool to let it slip through his fingers.

Her anxieties were slowly but surely beginning to melt away. She would always hate hospitals. They would always have that association for her. But somehow, this time, things felt different.

Different because she knew Rhuaridh had her back.

If she needed a minute—if her heart started racing or her breathing stuck somewhere inside her chest—she didn't need to hide it or pretend it was something else entirely. And the weird thing was that none of those things had actually happened.

Maybe it was Bill, the older man, who'd distracted her completely. In a lucid moment he'd just told her about his wife dying fifteen years before and how much it had broken his heart. Then he'd started to gently sing a Christmas carol they'd loved together. Kristie had joined in and when, a few moments later, he'd become confused and panicky, she'd taken his hand and reassured him about where he was, who he was, and what he was doing there.

This could be her. This could be Rhuaridh. This could be anyone that she knew and loved. No one knew what path lay ahead for them, and if she could give Bill a few moments of reassurance and peace then she would.

Rhuaridh came over and placed a warm hand on her shoulder. 'I've just finished. Do you have some more people to film?'

She shook her head. 'Gerry's looking tired. I think we've done enough today. We'll come back tomorrow and finish then.'

Rhuaridh gave a nod. 'Okay. The snow's got a bit thicker since yesterday. We might be able to scrounge up a few snowballs. Are you game?'

She wrinkled her nose. 'Game? What does that mean?'

He laughed. 'It's like a challenge. It means are you ready to do a particular action—like making snowballs.'

Now she understood. She took a few minutes to say goodbye to Bill, then joined Rhuaridh. 'Okay, then, I'm game.'

Gerry joined them outside, and grabbed the car keys while they plotted. The hospital grounds were large, with a grassy forecourt lined with trees.

'Why go anywhere else?' asked Kristie. She zipped up her new red winter jacket—which would never see the light of day in LA. She kicked at the thick snow on the ground. 'Let's just have our snowball fight here.' She put her hands on her hips and looked around, her breath steaming in the air in front of her. 'Or maybe we should start with a snowman. I've always wanted to build a snowman.'

Rhuaridh pulled some gloves out of his pocket. Kristie winced. Gloves. She'd forgotten about gloves. He walked closer. 'Did you forget the most essential tool for playing with snow?'

She grimaced, hating to start on the back foot. 'Maybe.'

He handed his gloves over. 'Here, use mine.'

She grinned. 'Doesn't you being a gentleman give me an unfair advantage?'

His eyes gleamed. He leaned forward, his lips brushing against the side of her face as he whispered in her ear. 'Yeah, but that would only count if I thought you might actually win.'

'That's fighting talk.' She gave him her sternest glare but she knew he was teasing.

He nodded. 'It is. So let's start. First to make a snowman wins.'

She looked across at the wide snow-covered lawn and wagged her finger encased in the thick gloves. 'We split this straight down the middle. Don't try and steal my snow.'

'Your snow?'

'Absolutely. This is *my* snow.' She gave him a wary nod. 'I'm the guest.'

'You are, aren't you?' He bent down and scooped some of the snow into his bare hands. 'I haven't told you, have I?'

She frowned. 'Told me what?'

'I might have a bit of a competitive streak. Go!' Something streaked across the dark sky towards her, hitting her squarely on the shoulder and splattering up into her face.

She choked for a second as Rhuaridh's deep laugh rang across the night air. He didn't waste any time. He ran straight into the middle of his patch and started trying to pack snow together.

She shook the snow off her hair and out of her face. 'Cheat! I'll get you for that.'

'Keep up!' he shouted over his shoulder.

She didn't waste any time, running to her own patch of snow and trying to pack it like Rhuaridh was doing. After a few minutes she had pressed enough together to form a giant snowball that she could start rolling across the grass to make it bigger. She couldn't hide her delight. Within a few minutes she was out of breath. Pushing snow was harder than she could ever have imagined.

She looked up. Rhuaridh was making it look so easy. Ratfink.

She kept going, loving the whole experience of being in the snow. Before long she had a medium-sized snowball, just about big enough to be a body.

Rhuaridh had already positioned his in the middle of the green and was rolling another. She ran to catch up, ignoring the fact hers already looked a bit smaller than his.

If he thought he had a competitive edge, he had nothing on her.

She stopped for a moment, distracted by seeing him blow on his hands for a few seconds. Just watching him gave her a little thrill. His dark hair, which always looked as if it just about needed cutting, his broad shoulders and long legs. Jeans suited him—though she'd never say it out loud. Even from here she could see the deep concentration on his face as he went back to rolling the second ball for the snowman's head. It gave her the opening she needed. She pulled together her first small snowball and threw it straight at him. It landed right at his feet.

He looked up and smiled. 'Given up already? What's happened to your snowman?'

'I've taken pity on you,' she said quickly, not wanting to admit that she'd no idea how, if she rolled a second ball of snow, she'd actually get it on top of the snowman. She grinned and grabbed some more snow, trying her best to shape a snowball and throw it at him. But it seemed she didn't quite have the technique and it disintegrated in mid-air.

'Seems like you LA girls need some snow

training,' he said as he strode towards her. He was laughing at her.

She tried again then started to laugh too when it didn't quite work. 'What is it? Do they teach Scottish kids how to make a snowball at birth?'

He shook his head. 'Much earlier. We learn in the womb. It's a survival skill.'

He was right next to her, his tall frame standing over her. She dusted off the gloves and looked up, taking a step closer. She wanted to hold her breath, to stop steam appearing between them. His hair was in front of his deep blue eyes—and they were fixed on hers. Behind him was the backdrop of the navy sky speckled with stars, followed by the snow-covered outline of the cottage hospital. Right now, it felt like being on a Christmas card.

He lifted one hand and touched the side of her cheek, his cold finger made her jump, and they both laughed. 'Red looks good on you,' he said huskily.

'Does it?' She couldn't help it, she stepped forward. She just couldn't resist. It was as if there was a magnet, pulling them together. They were already close but this removed the gap between them. His other hand went instantly to her waist.

He gave a little tug at the scarf around her neck. 'I guess I should say it now.'

She swore her heart gave a jump. 'Say what?'

His cold finger traced a line up her neck, and across her lips. Teasing her.

His head dipped down towards her. 'It's a little early.'

Yip, her heart had forgotten how to beat steadily.

'Early for what?' she whispered.

He pulled something out of his pocket. She recognised it. It was plastic, green and white, slightly bent, and had come from the decoration box in the hospital.

'What are you doing?' she asked.

'This,' he said, 'is mistletoe. And I thought it was time to say Merry Christmas and introduce you to the Scottish tradition.'

She slid her arms around his waist as her smile grew wider. 'And what tradition might that be?'

His lips lowered towards hers. 'The one of kissing under the mistletoe.'

His lips weren't as cold as his hands and the

connection between them sent a little shock-wave through her body. Last time they'd kissed had been in his front room. It had been comfortable. Warm. And had felt so right.

This was what she'd been waiting for. This had been the thing that had teased in her dreams for the last two months. Expectation was everything. And Rhuaridh Gillespie was meeting every expectation she'd ever had.

Because kissing the hot Highland doc was like standing in a field full of fireworks. And if things got any hotter, they'd light up the entire island.

CHAPTER NINE

January

'IT'S DYNAMITE! WHY didn't you tell me you two were an item?'

'What?' Kristie rubbed her eyes.

'The film. The backdrop of snow. The two of you silhouetted outside the hospital, kissing. The public will die for this. I tell you, once this goes out, you'll have any job that you want. What *do* you want? A talk show? More reporting? How about something fun, like a game show?'

For the briefest of seconds she felt a surge of excitement. Louie was telling her she could have her pick of jobs. How long had she waited to hear those words?

But her stomach gave a flip and she tried to mentally replay what he'd said.

Her voice cut across his as he kept talking. She could almost feel the blood drain from her body. 'What do you mean—the kiss? The silhouette?'

'You and Gerry must have planned that. Tell me you planned it. It couldn't have been more photogenic. I guarantee you that someone will put that picture on a calendar next year.'

Dread swept over her. 'Is that what you think of me? That I *planned* to kiss Rhuaridh?'

'Best career move ever,' came Louie's prompt reply.

Now she was sitting bolt upright in bed. They'd caught the last ferry to Arran the night before and when she'd gone to Rhuaridh's cottage there had been no one home—not even Mac.

She hadn't managed to see the last lot of the footage. Gerry had some excuse about technical issues. Now she knew why. She'd kill him. She'd kill him with her bare hands.

She stumbled out of bed, her feet getting caught in the blankets. For a few seconds she blinked then glanced at her watch. It was still dark outside. Shouldn't it be daytime? She kept the phone pressed to her ear as she walked over and drew back the curtains, flinching back at the thick dark clouds and mist.

'Don't you dare use that footage. I've not seen it. And I didn't agree to it being used.'

'Of course you did,' said Louie quickly. 'It's in your contract.'

'*Please*, Louie.' She didn't know whether to shout or burst into tears. She'd try either if she thought they might work. 'I let you get away with using my sick footage. But not this stuff. It's not fair on me. And it's not fair on Rhuaridh.'

'Oh, it's not fair on Rhuaridh?' Louie's voice rose and Kristie knew his eyebrows had just shot upwards. 'Well, it's pretty obvious that you like him now. But just remember, you have a job to do. And don't forget exactly what he's getting in return for us filming. And anyway, by the end of all this neither of you two will need to work. You'll spend the next few years touting yourselves around the talk shows. The public will *love* this.'

Her heart plummeted. Everything she'd felt about the kiss, the anticipation, the expectation, the longing, and the electricity—the whole moment had stayed in her mind like some delicious kind of dream. But now it seemed tarnished. It seemed contrived and unreal. She sagged down onto her bed. She'd wanted to keep the kiss to herself. She'd wanted that intensely personal moment to remain between her and Rhuaridh. Because that's the way it should be. Her perfect Christmas kiss.

'Gotta go,' Louie said quickly. 'Got another call. Try and catch another kiss on film—or maybe have a fight. That could really kick the figures up.'

The phone clicked. He was gone.

Her brain was spinning. She'd planned to get up this morning and put the new clothes on she'd bought to meet Rhuaridh. She had the whole thing pictured in her head. The checked pinafore she'd picked up that almost looked tartan, along with the thick black tights and black sweater—again clothing she'd never have a chance to wear in LA. It was amazing how a few days in Scotland a month had started to change her wardrobe. She'd never had much use for chunky tights, warm clothing and thick winter jackets. She even had a few coloured scarves, gloves and hats.

Now the pinafore hanging over the back of the chair in the room seemed to be mocking her. Her jaw tightened. She grabbed yesterday's jeans and shirt, pulling them on in two minutes flat, and marched across the hall towards Gerry's room. She couldn't hide the fact she was anything other than mad.

'You filmed us? You filmed us and you didn't tell me?' She had burst straight through the door—not even knocking.

Gerry was standing with his back to her, the camera at his shoulder. He spun around and swayed. She stepped forward to continue her tirade but the words stuck somewhere in her throat. Gerry's skin was glassy. She couldn't even describe the colour. White, translucent, with even a touch of grey.

Even before she got a chance to get any more words out, Gerry's eyes rolled and he pitched forward onto the bed.

'Gerry!' she yelled, grabbing at him and fumbling him round onto his back. She knelt on the bed and shook both his shoulders. But his eyes remained closed.

She tried to remember what she'd seen on TV. She felt around for a pulse, not finding anything at the neck but eventually finding a weak, thready pulse at his wrist. She squinted at his chest. Was he breathing? It seemed very slow.

She grabbed her phone and automatically pressed Rhuaridh's number. He answered after the second ring. His voice was bright. 'Kristie, are you—?'

'Help. I need help. It's Gerry. He's collapsed at the bed and breakfast we're staying in.'

She could hear the change in his tone immediately, almost like he'd flicked a switch to go into doctor mode. 'Kristie, where is he?'

'On the bed.' She was leaning over Gerry, watching him intently.

'Was there an accident?'

'What? No. He just collapsed.'

'Is he breathing?'

She paused, eyes fixed on Gerry's chest. 'I… I think so.'

'Has he got a pulse?'

'Yes, but it's not strong…and it's not regular.'

'Kristie, I'm getting in the car. Pam has phoned for the ambulance. Which B and B are you at?'

She glanced over her shoulder to find the name on the folder on the bedside table, reciting the name to Rhuaridh.

'I'll be five minutes. Shout for help. Get

someone to stay with you, and tell them to make sure the front door is open.'

It was the longest five minutes of her life. When Rhuaridh appeared at the door, at the same time as the ambulance crew, she wanted to throw her arms around him.

She moved out of the way as they quickly assessed Gerry, then moved him onto a stretcher. Gerry seemed to have regained consciousness, although his colour remained terrible. She darted around to the side of the bed and grabbed his hand. 'Why didn't you tell me you didn't feel well?' she asked.

He shook his head and as he made that movement, parts of her brain sprang to life. The way his colour hadn't been great the last few months, his indigestion, his tiredness.

A tear sprang to her eye. She'd missed it. She should have told him to get checked out. But she'd been too preoccupied with herself, too occupied with the show—and with Rhuaridh—to properly look out for her colleague.

Rhuaridh pulled some bottles from his bag and found two separate tablets. 'Gerry,' he said firmly. 'I need you to swallow these two tablets. It's important. Can you do that for me?'

One of the ambulance crew handed him a glass of water with a straw. 'C'mon, mate, let's see if you can manage these.'

After a few seconds Gerry grimaced then managed to swallow down the tablets. Rhuaridh opened Gerry's shirt and quickly attached a monitor to his chest.

Kristie reached out and touched his shoulder. 'Gerry, I'm sorry, please be okay.'

Gerry's eyes flickered open. 'Hey,' he said shakily. 'Remember the camera.' He gave a crooked smile. 'Don't want to miss anything.' His eyes closed again and Kristie felt herself moved aside as the ambulance crew member reached for the stretcher.

She gulped then grabbed the car keys as Rhuaridh turned towards her. 'What's wrong?' she whispered.

Rhuaridh's voice was low. 'I think he's had a heart attack. I'll be able to confirm it at the hospital.'

She nodded as a tear rolled down her cheek.

'Hey,' he said softly as he picked up his bag. His other hand reached up and brushed her tear away. 'Don't cry. We'll get things sorted.'

'Doc?' A voice carried from outside the door.

One of the ambulance crew stuck his head back inside. 'We might have a problem.'

He was stuck between trying to reassure Kristie and trying to reassure himself.

The weather was abysmal. No helicopter could land on Arran or take off in the next few hours. It seemed he was it.

This happened. This was island life. Thankfully it didn't happen too often, but in the modern age lots of people didn't really understand what living on an island meant.

Kristie was pacing outside as Rhuaridh read Gerry's twelve-lead ECG and rechecked his observations. Normally people with a myocardial infarction would be transported to hospital and treated within two hours. But those two hours were ticking past quickly and Gerry had no hope of reaching a cardiac unit.

Most people with this condition would end up in a cardiac theatre, with an angiogram and stent inserted to open up the blocked vessel. But there was no specialised equipment like that on Arran.

There were monitoring facilities and Gerry was currently attached to a cardiac monitor in one of the side rooms with an extra nurse called in to observe him closely for the next twenty-four hours.

Kristie couldn't stop pacing. He hated to see how worried she was, but the truth was he couldn't give her the guarantee she so desperately needed—that Gerry would be fine.

Rhuaridh put down the phone after talking to one of the consultants in Glasgow. Emergency situations called for emergency treatment.

'What's happening?' Kristie was at his side in an instant.

He ran his fingers through his hair. 'Bloods and ECG confirm it. Gerry's had a massive heart attack. If he was on the mainland he'd go to Theatre to get the vessel cleared and probably have a stent put in to try and stop it happening again.'

It seemed she knew where this conversation would go. 'But here?'

'But here I've given him the first two drugs that should help, and now we'll need to do things the more old-fashioned way and give him an IV of a drug that should break up the clot.'

She frowned. 'Why don't you still just do that? It sounds better than Theatre.'

He gave a slow nod. He had to phrase this carefully. 'Studies show the other way is better. But as that isn't an option, this is the only one we have.'

'That doesn't sound good.' Her voice cracked.

Rhuaridh put his hand on her arm. 'It takes an hour for the treatment to go in, then we have to monitor him carefully. There can be some side-effects, that's why we've called an extra nurse in to monitor Gerry all day and overnight.'

Kristie's head flicked from side to side. 'Right, where can I stay?'

He tried not to smile. He knew she would do this. 'You can stay with me. I'm going to have to stay overnight too. We'll pull a few chairs into one of the other rooms close by. Miriam, the nurse, can give me a shout if she needs me.'

He looked down at her white knuckles gripping the camera in her hand. 'What are you going to do with that?'

She took a few breaths as if she were thinking about it, then she lifted her chin and looked at him. 'I'm going to do Gerry's job. I'll film it.'

There was something in her eyes that struck him as strange. 'Are you okay?'

Her jaw was tight. 'If Gerry was the one out here, he would film. He told me back at the B and B.' She nodded as if she was processing a few things. 'And I'll film you. You can explain what a heart attack is and what the medicines are that you've given Gerry.' She paused for the briefest of seconds then added, 'Then you can talk about the weather and why we can't leave. I'll ask you a few questions about that.'

He tilted his head to the side. What was wrong with Kristie? Something just seemed a little...off. He understood she was worried about her colleague. Maybe this was her way of coping—to just throw herself into work.

He gave a cautious nod. 'Of course we can do an interview. But give me a bit of time. I'm going to set up the IV with Miriam and have a chat with Gerry.'

She pressed her lips together and swung the camera up onto her shoulder. 'Carry on. I'll capture what I can.'

Just as he'd finally managed to get used to Gerry constantly hovering in the background with a camera, now everything was flipped on its head and Kristie hovering with a camera was something else entirely. Initially he'd found Gerry's filming intrusive, and probably a bit unnecessary. But Kristie's? That was just unnerving. Gerry had an ability to be unnoticeable and virtually silent. Now he was constantly aware of the scent of Kristie drifting from behind him and the noise of her footsteps on the hospital floor.

Where Gerry had felt like a ghost, Kristie was more like a neon light.

And things were certainly illuminating. It turned out Gerry had been harbouring a history of niggling indigestion and heaviness in his arms and a constant feeling of tiredness. Trouble was, Gerry had worked out himself that all the signs were pointing to cardiac trouble—but instead of seeking treatment he'd kept quiet, out of fear of losing his job.

Rhuaridh wasn't there to judge. Healthcare and insurance in the US was completely different from healthcare in the UK.

He turned to speak to Kristie just in time to notice a big fat tear slide down her cheek. Her eyes were fixed on Gerry's pale face as he lay with his eyes closed on the hospital bed, surrounded by flashing monitors and beeping IVs.

Something inside him clenched. This was her

worst nightmare. Of course it was. She hated hospitals and now she was forcing herself to stay to be with Gerry. He knew in his heart that any suggestion he made about her leaving would fall on deaf ears. Rhuaridh slid his arm around her shoulders and pulled her towards him. 'You okay?'

She shook her head then rested it on his shoulder. 'I was mad at him. I went across to his room to shout at him.'

Rhuaridh tilted his head towards her. 'Why on earth did you want to shout at Gerry? You two seem to get on so well. You complement each other.'

She hesitated for a second then pulled a face. 'If I tell you why I was mad, you might get mad too.'

Rhuaridh shook his head. He had no idea what she was talking about. 'Okay, I feel as if I missed part of the conversation here.'

Her eyes lowered, her hands fumbling in her lap. Her voice was sad when she spoke. 'I found out Gerry filmed us kissing outside the hospital in December. I didn't know. He didn't say a word to me. And now my producer, Louie, has seen it, and loves it, so it's going to be in the next episode of the show, no matter how much I begged him not to use it.'

For the first time since she'd got here Rhuaridh felt distinctively uncomfortable. He didn't actually care about being filmed kissing Kristie. What he did care about was the fact she didn't seem to want anyone else to know. All those previous thoughts that he'd pushed away rushed into his head. Why would a girl like Kristie be interested in a guy from a Scottish island?

He took a deep breath and said the words he really didn't want to. 'What's wrong with us kissing?'

Her head turned sharply towards his. 'It's private. It's not something I want to share with the world.'

She was looking at him as if he should understand this. But his stomach was still twisting. His brain was sparking everywhere. He was looking at this woman in a new way. A way that told him she could easily break his heart.

He'd kind of shut himself off from the world since he'd come to Arran—focusing on work had seemed easier than realising he might never get the opportunity to meet someone to share his life with. And even though he knew things were ridiculous and completely improbable, even the fact that he'd thought about Kristie in that context had meant that he'd finally started to open himself up a little again. But it seemed he couldn't have timed things worse.

'We were in a public place,' he said carefully. 'That isn't so private.'

For a millisecond he might have been annoyed with Gerry—just like he had been in the beginning, questioning everything they filmed and the ethics behind it.

But Kristie had already told him. She needed this show to be a hit. If she didn't want the world to know they'd kissed, then at least part of him could be relieved she wasn't playing him.

She looked wounded by his words, her hand flew up to her chest. 'But it's private to me,' she said empathically.

He leaned forward, looking into those blue eyes and then whispering in her ear, 'Kristie, I don't care if the world knows we're kissing.' And he meant it. He glanced at Gerry on the bed. They still didn't know how this would all turn out for Gerry. If he had medical insurance he'd get shipped home once his treatment was complete. But chances were Rhuaridh wouldn't see him again anytime soon. Gerry might not be fit enough to travel like he had been.

He had to admire the canny old rogue. He'd seen the opportunity to film and taken it. Something flashed into Rhuaridh's head. Something he hadn't really processed earlier.

'Gerry asked you to film—and you did. We don't know how this is going to play out yet, Kristie.' He was serious. The IV drug Gerry was currently on could cause heart arrhythmias. It could also lead to small clots being thrown off while the heart was trying to re-perfuse. There were no guarantees right now. 'I'm not sure this is footage you should use.'

He left the words hanging in the air.

She blinked and her body gave a tremble. When she spoke her voice was shaky, 'I'm a terrible person. You know I want Gerry to be okay, don't you?'

He nodded and she continued, 'And I was still angry when he asked me to start filming, so I just automatically did. I've left the camera running at times without actually being behind it. I'm not even sure exactly what's been shot.'

Rhuaridh slid his hand over hers. 'I know what you're thinking. You need to take a breath. Take a moment. If Gerry is fine, then you've covered his work. You can show what happens to people in an island community when there's no possibility of getting off the island. This is a fact of life here. Gerry's had an alternative treatment for his heart attack. We hope it will work. If it does, you have footage.' He squeezed her hand. 'If it doesn't, then you stay some extra days and we'll shoot something else.'

He was trying to give her an alternative. The last thing he wanted was for her to be forced to use footage that would prove to be heartbreaking for her. He whispered again. 'No one needs know it's there.'

She shook her head. 'But it is. Our cameras don't need to go back to the studio to be uploaded. Everything uploads automatically to our server. Even if I don't want to use it, Louie probably will.'

'Surely he's not that heartless? You told me he was the guy that held your hand while you were at the hospital.' He leaned forward. 'Footage of us kissing? That's nothing. But if something happens to Gerry? No way. He couldn't use that. He wouldn't use that.' Rhuaridh wasn't quite sure who he was trying to convince. Her or himself.

She leaned back in against his shoulder and put her hand up on his chest. 'I hope so,' she whispered in reply, as both of their eyes fixed on the pulse, pulse, pulse of Gerry's monitor.

CHAPTER TEN

February

TRAVELLING WITH SOMEONE else felt all wrong. Thea was nice enough, but clearly obsessed. She had around one hundred Scottish travel books and couldn't seem to understand there wasn't time to drive around all the rest of Scotland before they got the ferry to Arran. It seemed she hadn't quite grasped the size of Scotland, or the terrain. By the time they docked in Arran, Kristie had a full-blown migraine.

The last few days at the helpline had been hard. Someone had called and kept hanging up after a few minutes. Every time it had happened, Kristie's thoughts flooded back to her sister. This could be someone like Jess. Someone who needed to be heard but couldn't find the words.

She'd struggled with it so much but she dealt with her feelings by continuing to work on the book she'd started writing a couple of months before. It had been years since she'd tried to write things. Last time she'd done this she'd been in college. But all of that had been pushed aside as her course work had taken priority. Now this story seemed to be shaping itself. All of it was fiction. None of it was based on a real person. Instead, it was an amalgamation of years of experiences. But it all felt real to Kristie. Even though this show was the thing the whole world was excited about, this story was the thing that kept her awake at night— that, and thinking of a hot Highland doc.

She'd also had over a thousand social media messages today alone. Since the kiss had been shown, her social media presence had erupted even more than before. Her conversations with Rhuaridh had continued. He'd been hit with just as many messages as she had—more, probably. And he was feeling a bit shell-shocked by it all. But Rhuaridh seemed able to pull his professional face into place and use his job as a protective shield.

She looked up just in time to meet the glare of an elegant-looking woman with gleaming dark brown hair. She looked out of place on the Arran ferry in her long wine-coloured wool coat, matching lipstick and black high heels. Kristie frowned. Why on earth would that woman be glaring at her?

'Will he be waiting for you at the dock? Should I film that?' Thea asked. Kristie started at Thea's voice and turned just in time to catch Thea shooting her a suspicious look. 'And this thing—it is real? Or is it all just made up for the camera? I have to admit I'm kind of curious.'

Kristie was more than a little stunned. 'You think it's fake?'

Thea was still talking. 'I mean, let's just say I'm asking in principle, because—let's face it—he is *hot*.'

A surge of jealousy swept through Kristie. 'You think Rhuaridh is *hot*?' She said the words almost in disbelief.

Thea threw back her head and laughed. 'Oh, honey, the whole world thinks he's hot.'

Now she wasn't just jealous. Now she was mad. Rhuaridh Gillespie was hers. She could picture herself as a three-year-old stamping her foot. Very mature.

And still Thea kept talking. Did the woman ever shut up? 'And anyway, you're from LA, he's from—what is it called again? Arran? How's that ever gonna work? He might as well be on the moon. I mean, let's face it, in a few months you won't be getting paid to come here any more. I bet these flights cost a small fortune.'

A horrible sensation swept over Kristie. She'd always known this—it's not like she was stupid. But she'd tried not to think about it.

The horn sounded as the boat docked, the sound ricocheting through Kristie's head. She winced and stood up. 'Come on,' she growled at Thea.

Her heart gave a leap as she pulled into the car park of the GP surgery. Rhuaridh was standing outside, waiting for her, his thick blue parka zipped up against the biting wind.

Thea let out a sound kind of like a squeak as Kristie jumped out of the car and ran towards him. She couldn't help it. Four weeks was just too long. Rhuaridh dropped a kiss on her nose and wrapped his arm around her. 'What's the update on Gerry?' he asked straight away.

She gave a sigh. 'Good, but not so good. He's started cardiac rehab classes and is making some progress. He's tired. I think he's frustrated that things are taking longer than he hoped. He's been assured he should make a good recovery, but just has to show some patience.' She pulled a face. 'And the TV channel won't cover his travel insurance until he's been signed off as fit by the doctor. And, to be honest, I think that will take a few months.'

The way Rhuaridh nodded made her realise that he'd known this all along—even if she hadn't. He leaned forward and touched her cheek with his finger. 'You okay? You look tired.'

'I am.' She glanced sideways over her shoulder. 'Thea—I'll introduce you to her in a sec—is exhausting. My head is thumping.'

He paused for a second, giving Thea, who already had the camera on her shoulder, a quick wave. 'And the next show?'

Kristie let out another sigh. Maybe she was more tired than she'd thought. 'The show is going out with Gerry as the star and you and I as background footage. Gerry's fine about it.'

'And are you?'

'I guess I should be happy we're not as front

and centre this time. But we're still there. The camera was running at the hospital and it's caught us sitting together, holding hands.'

'I can live with that.' It was as if he chose those words carefully.

She met his gaze, ignoring the way her hair was whipping around her face in the wind. 'So can I.' She couldn't help the small smile that appeared on her face. There was just something about being around Rhuaridh. Not only did he make her heart beat at a million miles a second, he was also her comfort zone. Her place.

She leaned forward and rested her head against his chest for a second. 'Kristie?' he said.

Although she'd told him about her sister, she'd never got round to telling him about the helpline. Things were playing on her mind. She needed a chance to talk to him—but she wanted to do that when they were alone.

She lifted her head. 'Can we go to the pub tonight for dinner?' Tonight was only a couple of hours away. She could wait that long.

'Of course.' He nodded. She watched as he painted a smile on his face and put his hand out towards Thea. 'Gerry, you've changed a little,' he joked. 'Welcome to Arran.'

* * *

Three hours later they finally had some peace and quiet. Even though the pub was busy, they were tucked in a little nook at the back where no one could hear them talk.

Rob, the barman, had just brought over their plates of steaming food, steak pie for Rhuaridh and fish for Kristie. Rhuaridh lifted his fork to his mouth and halted.

Kristie followed his gaze. The elegant woman from the boat was crossing the pub, heading directly towards their table. Every head in the room turned as she passed, her wool coat now open, revealing a form-fitting black dress underneath. She was easily the best-dressed woman in the room and she knew it.

Kristie's skin prickled. She could sense trouble. Rhuaridh looked almost frozen as the woman approached.

Kristie tilted her head, pretending she felt totally at ease. 'Can I help you?'

The woman looked down her nose at Kristie. For all her elegance, she wasn't half as pretty when she was sneering at someone. 'Oh, the American.' She said the words as if Kristie were some kind of disease.

Years of experience across cutthroat TV shows meant that Kristie was more than prepared for any diva behaviour. She gave her most dazzling smile. 'I'm afraid you have me at a disadvantage. Who are you?' The words were amiable enough, but Kristie knew exactly how to deliver them. The implication of 'not being important enough to know' emanated from her every pore.

There was a flash of anger in the woman's eyes but Rhuaridh broke in. 'Kristie, this is Zoe.'

'Zoe?'

The woman straightened her shoulders. 'Zoe Brackenridge. Rhuaridh and I are...' a calculating smile appeared on her lips '...very good, old friends.'

The ex. It was practically stamped on her forehead. But Kristie wasn't easily bested.

Zoe seemed to dismiss her, turning her attention to Rhuaridh. 'Rhuaridh, do you think we could go back to the cottage? I think we need to have a private chat.'

'I'm not quite sure there's room enough for three,' said Kristie quickly. Too quickly, in fact, she was in danger of letting this woman make her lose her cool.

But it seemed that Rhuaridh had limited patience too. 'What are you doing on Arran, Zoe? I thought you hated the place.' His gaze was steely.

There was a tiny flicker in the woman's cheek. She wasn't unnerved. She was angry. She looked Rhuaridh straight in the eye, 'Like I said, we need to talk.'

'We talked some time ago. I think you said everything you needed to.'

Zoe leaned forward and touched Rhuaridh's arm, leaving her hand there. Kristie resisted the temptation to stab her with her fork. 'Rhuaridh, I'm sure there are some things we could catch up on.'

'Like what?'

Kristie almost choked. She'd never heard Rhuaridh be that rude before. Funnily enough, she kind of liked it.

Now Zoe was starting to show some signs of frustration. 'I think we have a lot of things to catch up on. One of the consultants I'm working with was enquiring about you—there could be a job opportunity in Glasgow. It would be perfect for you.' She looked over her shoulder. 'Get you away from this island. Now you've done that show, you should be able to recruit someone else for here. Get your career back on track. Get your life back on track.'

Rhuaridh stood up, his dinner untouched, and reached out for Kristie's hand. 'You've watched the show?'

Kristie felt as if she'd been catapulted back into high school. This seemed like teenage behaviour. Rhuaridh had never really talked about the relationship he'd had with Zoe, but in Kristie's head she could see Zoe watching the show, seeing how captivated the world was with Rhuaridh, and realising exactly what she'd let go. Now she'd shown up like some high school prom queen back to claim her king.

Zoe rolled her eyes, then settled her gaze on Kristie. It was distinctly disapproving. 'It doesn't exactly show you in the best light.' She waved her hand. 'And as for that title...' She gave a shudder and touched his shoulder. 'I think it's time a friend helped you get back to where you should be.'

Kristie ground her teeth. Did this woman even know how condescending she sounded?

But she didn't get a chance to say anything. Rhuaridh stepped up right in front of the woman.

He stood there for a few seconds. Zoe cast Kristie a triumphant glance that was short-lived. Rhuaridh spoke in a low voice. 'Let me be clear. We don't have anything to talk about. And you've just rudely interrupted dinner between me…' he paused for the briefest of seconds '…and my girlfriend.'

It was like someone had sucked the air out of her lungs. *Girlfriend.* She liked that word. She liked it a lot.

'Goodbye, Zoe,' he finished as he gave Kristie's hand a tug and pulled her with him as he headed to the door, leaving some money on the bar. 'Sorry about dinner,' he muttered as he kept walking.

She ignored her empty stomach as she cast a look over her shoulder. Zoe looked stunned. It was probably her best look.

'Beans on toast,' said Rhuaridh. 'Fine dining. The staple diet of most Scottish students.'

Kristie raised her eyebrows at him. 'I think

we could have got away with taking the plates. No one would have noticed.'

He let out a sigh. She hadn't said a word in the car back to the cottage. It was as if she knew he needed some time to sort out his head. He couldn't believe Zoe had turned up here. There had been a few random emails that he hadn't replied to. But he would never have expected her to show up in the place she'd shown so much contempt for.

There had always been a side to Zoe that hadn't exactly been complimentary—one she tried to keep hidden. Zoe, at heart, was competitive. Whether that was in her career, in her love life, or in her finances. And it was the 'at heart' part that annoyed him most.

He'd been deluged with messages from every direction. Even though he still hadn't watched the show, he couldn't fail to notice its impact. Zoe's competitive edge must be cursing right now. She wasn't here really because she regretted her actions or her words. No, she was here because she wanted a bit of the limelight. This wasn't an act of love. This was an act of ambition.

Kristie pressed her lips together as she picked

up her plate and walked over to the sofa. It was clear her mind was somewhere else.

'I'm not sure what you and Thea have planned for footage for this month's filming. I imagine Thea will need to find her way around the surgery and hospital for now so I've not scheduled anything in particular. But I've arranged for filming in the school to happen next month,' he said quickly, trying to pull her away from whatever was giving her that pained expression. 'There's a whole host of immunisations coming up. They're handled by the nurse immunisation team, but I generally try to go along in case there are any issues.'

'What kind of issues?'

'There are usually a few fainters. The odd child who might have a panic attack. Consents are all done before we get there, and all the children's medical histories have been checked.'

'Mmm…okay.'

He put his plate down. 'Kristie, what did you want to talk about earlier?'

She pushed her plate away and pulled her legs up onto the sofa, turning to face him with her head on her hand. She gave her head a shake. 'I'm just tired. It's nothing.'

'It's not nothing. It's something. Tell me.'

She gulped. He could see her doing that so reached out and took her hand. After a few minutes she finally spoke. 'I told you about my sister. But what I didn't tell you was that after she died I contacted the helpline she'd phoned a few times and volunteered. The calls she made were short. She always disconnected. But I felt as if I wanted to do something.' She ran her other hand through her hair. 'I couldn't get it out of my head that when she'd been feeling low, the place she'd called was there, not me.'

Her voice started to tremble. 'And I realised that I could be that person at the end of the phone for someone else. So I volunteered, they trained me, and I've been manning the phone three times a month for the last few years.'

He'd listened carefully. He knew there was more.

'So what's wrong?'

She stared down at her hands. 'The last few nights, someone has been phoning, staying on the line for less than a minute then hanging up. I know that's what Jess did.' Her voice cracked. 'And I can't help but wonder if I'm failing them, just like I failed Jess.'

Rhuaridh didn't hesitate, he pulled her into his arms. 'You didn't fail your sister, Kristie, and you haven't failed this person either. They've called. They've got to take the decision to speak. Sometimes people call six or seven times before they pick up the courage to speak. All you can do is be there. All you can do is answer and let them know that you're prepared to listen whenever they want to speak.'

'But what if offering to listen isn't enough?' Her wide blue eyes were wet with tears.

His heart twisted in his chest. He could see just how desperate she was to save any other family from the pain she'd suffered. He could see just how much she wanted to help.

He put his hands at either side of her head. 'Kristie Nelson, you are a brilliant big-hearted person. But you have to accept that there are some things in this life we can't control—no matter how much we want to. All we can do... is the best that we can. I know that's hard to accept. But we have to. Otherwise the what-ifs will eat us up inside.'

He leaned forward and rested his head against hers. They stayed like that for the longest time. At first he could see the small pulse racing at the bottom of her neck, but the longer they stayed together, the more her body relaxed against his, and the more her breathing steadied and eased. He wanted to give her that space and time to gather her thoughts—just like he was gathering his.

She took another breath. 'There's more,' she said quietly.

'What?'

She licked her lips. 'These last few months I started working on something—a book.'

He was momentarily confused. 'A book?'

She nodded. 'It's fiction. But it's based on Jess, and what happens when a member of your family commits suicide. The impact it has on all those around. It's about a tight-knit family and a group of old high school friends. How they all second-guess themselves wondering if they could have done something—changed things—and how they have to learn to live and move on.'

He pulled back and looked at her, amazed. 'Wow, that sounds…incredible.' He reached forward and brushed back a strand of hair from her face. 'Can I read it?'

She looked surprised. 'Do you want to?'

'Of course. Now. Do you have it?'

A smile danced across her lips as she stood up and crossed the room, picking up her laptop. 'It's still in the early stages. There might be spelling mistakes—grammatical errors.'

He shook his head and held out his hands. 'I don't care. Just give it to me.'

He bent over the bright screen and started reading as she settled beside him.

Three hours later it was the early hours of the morning. Kristie's manuscript. It was beautiful, touching and from the heart. And it smacked of Kristie. Every word, every nuance had her unique stamp on it. He brushed a tear from his eye and nudged her. She'd fallen asleep on his shoulder.

'Kristie, wake up.' He gave her a shake and she rubbed her tired eyes.

'You've finished?'

He nodded and she bit her bottom lip. 'What did you think?'

He held out his hand. 'I think it's brilliant. It's heartbreaking. It's real. You have to finish this. *This* is what you should be doing, Kristie. This

is so important. I *felt* for every one of the people in this story. You have to get this out there.'

Her eyes sparkled. 'You think so? Really?'

He nodded. 'Without a doubt. You have a
gift as a writer. Do it. I believe in you. Once
an agent sees this, they'll snatch it up with both
hands.'

A smile danced across her lips. He could see
the impact his words were having. The fact he
believed in her ability to tell this story. It felt
like pieces of their puzzle were just slotting
into place.

He couldn't believe that Zoe had shown up
today. He'd never seen someone look so much
like a fish out of water. But it was almost as
if a shadow had been lifted off his shoulders.
She'd always intimated that Arran was less,
and he was less for being here. He'd compro-
mised his career and his life. And for a time
those thoughts had drip-dripped into his self-
conscious.

But tonight was like shining a bright light
on his life. Everything was clear for him. He
was exactly where he wanted to be, and with
the person he wanted to be with. Zoe's visit—
instead of unsettling him—had actually clari-

fied things for him. He didn't care about the distance between him and Kristie. He had no idea how things would play out. All he knew was that he wanted to think about the here and now. With her.

It was almost as if their brains were in accord. Kristie lifted her head and gave him a twinkling smile. 'I just remembered something you said tonight.'

'What?'

'Girlfriend, hey?' she said as she slid her arms around his neck.

His voice was low as his hands settled on her waist. 'I just remembered something you said too. I heard you tell her the cottage wasn't big enough for three,' he said as his lips danced across the skin on her neck. 'You made it sound like you were staying here.'

'Oh, I am.' She smiled as she pulled him down onto the sofa and made sure he knew exactly how things were.

CHAPTER ELEVEN

March

Don't get too comfortable. Miss LA will get just as sick of the place as any normal human would. How can smoggy hills compare to the glamour of Hollywood? Your success is just your fifteen minutes of fame. You should be asking yourself where your career will be in five years' time. That's what's important.

RHUARIDH SHOOK HIS head and deleted the email. It was sad, really. Zoe was trying to provoke a reaction from him and the truth was he felt nothing. He wasn't interested in her or in anything she had to say.

He looked out the window towards the hills. Were they smoggy? Maybe. Goatfell was covered at the top by some clouds. But Kristie had already said she wanted to climb it with him. Every time she visited she seemed a little more fascinated by Arran and wanted to see more. Her attitude was the complete opposite of Zoe's and that made him feel warm inside. She didn't see Arran as the last place on earth she wanted to visit—she might not want to ever stay here but when she was here, she made it seem like an adventure. And he'd take that.

He picked up the case he had ready to go to the high school. The immunisation team would be setting up right now and he'd arranged to meet Kristie and Thea there as they came straight off the first morning ferry. Chances were they'd be tired—they'd been travelling all night, but a delayed flight had caused them a few problems.

The local school was only a few minutes away. The whole place was buzzing. The immunisation team never failed to amaze him by how scarily organised they were. One of the nurses met him just as Thea burst through the door with her camera at the ready. 'Wait for me,' she shouted.

He shook his head and looked down at the list of children the nurse wanted him to give a quick review. Nothing much to worry about. Kristie stepped in behind Thea. Her cheeks flushed pink and her skin glowing. Every pair of eyes in the room turned towards them.

'Hey,' she said self-consciously, tugging at a strand of her hair.

'Hey,' he replied.

What he wanted to do was kiss her. But he didn't want to do it in front of an audience. As soon as the thought crossed his brain the irony struck him. Thanks to Gerry, the whole world had already seen them kiss.

Kristie slipped into professional mode. Interviewing a few of the nurses, watching the kids come in for their vaccinations and capturing a few of them on camera too.

Everything was going smoothly until one of the teachers came in, white-faced. 'Dr Gillespie. I need some help.' Rhuaridh didn't recognise him. He must be one of the supply teachers.

Rhuaridh looked up from where he was finishing talking to a child with a complicated medical history. 'Can it wait?'

The teacher shook his head. 'No, it definitely can't.' He was wringing his hands together and the worry lines across his forehead were deep.

Rhuaridh was on his feet in a few seconds.

Thea was still filming on the other side of the room, so Kristie followed Rhuaridh and the teacher up some stairs to the second floor of the school.

The teacher had started tugging at his shirt-sleeve. 'I don't know what to do. She's been up and down. Apparently her father died last year and the school has been worried about her. Sometimes she just walks out of class. But today—she's barricaded herself into one of the rooms. Her friend told us that she said she wanted to kill herself. To join her dad.'

Rhuaridh heard Kristie's footsteps falter behind him. He turned around and raised his hand. 'Maybe you should let me handle this.'

He could see the strain on her face, but didn't get a chance to say anything further as the teacher stopped in front of one of the rooms. 'Here,' he said. 'I've tried everything.'

'Is it Jill Masterton?' Rhuaridh asked. He knew everyone on the island—so unless someone new had just moved over, the only teenager he knew who had lost her father in the last year was Jill.

The teacher nodded. 'I've been talking to her

for the last half-hour. I didn't think she was serious. I just thought it was attention-seeking. But…but then she said some other stuff, and I realised…' he shook his head '…whatever it was I was saying just wasn't helping.'

Rhuaridh could see the stress on the teacher's face. 'Have you contacted her mum?'

He nodded. 'She's on the mainland, waiting to catch the first ferry back.'

Rhuaridh took a deep breath. He didn't know this girl well. He hadn't seen much of her in the surgery. He turned to the teacher. 'Do you have any guidance teachers or counsellors attached to the school?'

The teacher shook his head. 'I'm only temporary. I came to cover sick leave. The guidance teacher—you probably know her, Mary McInnes—had surgery on her ankle. She's not expected back for a few months.'

Of course. He should have remembered that. He ran his fingers through his hair. 'Has she told you anything at all?'

The teacher now tugged at his tie. It was clear he was feeling out of his depth. 'She won't speak to me at all. But she doesn't know me.

And the teachers that she does know haven't had any reply. Last time someone tried to speak to her she said if anyone else came she would jump out of the window.'

There was a nagging voice of doubt in Rhuaridh's head. He hadn't seen this young girl since he'd got back here. She wouldn't remember him at all. When he'd left the island she'd been barely a baby. He held out his hands. 'I'm a doctor. I can speak to her. But I'm not a psychiatrist, or a psychologist. I don't want to make anything worse. Particularly if she's already made threats.'

'Do you have any other counsellors on the island?' Kristie stepped forward. The teacher shook his head.

She put her hand on her chest. 'Then let me.' She turned to Rhuaridh. 'You know that I've been trained. Let me talk to her. Maybe I can relate. I lost someone I loved too, plus I understand what it's like to be a teenage girl.'

'I don't want you to be out of your depth,' he said quietly. He was thinking about her being upset the other week when the caller to the helpline wouldn't speak.

'I want to try,' she said determinedly.

Rhuaridh turned back to the teacher. 'Maybe we should wait. Maybe we should tell her that her mum is on her way back over on the ferry. Has anything else been happening in the school we should know about—any bullying?'

The teacher shrugged. 'I'm sorry. I just don't know. Nothing obvious.'

Rhuaridh let out a sigh. He was torn. Torn between looking after the girl behind the door and putting the woman he loved in a position of vulnerability.

There was so much at risk here, so much at stake. How would this affect Jill and Kristie if things didn't work out? What if Jill reacted to something that Kristie said—the impact on both could be devastating. He was so torn. He wanted to fix this himself—but he wasn't sure that he could. Maybe Jill would react better to a woman, particularly one who might understand her loss. Ahead of him was the closed door. It was symbolic really—demonstrating exactly how the young girl in there felt. He glanced from the panicked temporary teacher and the determined woman in front of him, his head juggling what was best for everyone. There was a hollow echo in his head.

* * *

Kristie straightened up. She'd had enough of this. Enough of waiting. He was trying to protect her—she got that. But she didn't need protection.

On the ferry on the way over here today, all she'd thought about was how much she wanted to see Rhuaridh. How much she wanted to be in his arms. For the last four weeks she'd started to dream in Technicolor—and the dreams didn't just include Rhuaridh, they also included this place. Arran, with its lush green countryside, hills and valleys, and surrounding stormy seas. Even though she'd had a dozen job offers now and enough money in the bank to pay the bills for a while, her love of TV was definitely waning. The book she'd started writing had taken on a life of its own. Rhuaridh's encouragement had meant the world to her, and after that the words had just seemed to flow even easier. She'd shown it to Louie, who'd shown it to another friend who was a literary agent. The agent had offered representation already. It was almost like her world had shifted, shaping her future. And the one thing she'd been sure of was that her heart was leading the charge. Could she think about a life in Scotland? She hadn't really considered things. Would she be able to walk away from her TV career, and her work with the helpline?

She swallowed and turned to both men. 'I'm going to do this.'

She walked up to the door and stood close, trying to think of the best way to appeal to Jill. Kids were all over social media right now. Maybe she should try the *you-might-know-me* approach?

She gave the door a gentle rap with her knuckles. 'Jill, it's Kristie Nelson. You know, from the TV show? I've come to talk to you.'

She could hear sobbing inside the room. The kind that made the bottom fall out of her stomach. 'I don't want to talk to anyone.'

Kristie leaned her head back against the door, trying to think like a teenager these days. Her head was still in the social media zone. Their life revolved around social media. She pulled out her phone and did a search for Jill. Sure enough, it only took seconds to find her. Her online profile had a few selfies, and a few older pictures that showed a little girl laughing, sitting on her father's knee. It made her heart pang.

'How are you feeling?' she started.

'How do you think I'm feeling?' came the angry shout.

Good. She'd had another reply. Her main goal now was to keep Jill talking.

'I know about your dad, Jill. I know how sad you're feeling. Do you want to talk? Because I'm here. I'm here to listen to you.'

The sobs got more exasperated. 'How can you know how I'm feeling? How can you know what's in my head? Have you lost your dad?'

Kristie turned around and slid down the door so she was leaning against it. She may as well get comfortable. She wanted Jill to know that she was there to stay—there to listen. 'I've lost both of my parents,' she answered quietly. 'And I lost my sister three years ago. And I think about her every single day and the fact she's not here. And sometimes it catches me unawares—like when I see something I know she'd like and I can't show it to her, or when I hear something that makes me laugh and I can't pick up the phone and tell her.'

There was silence for a few seconds then she heard a noise. Jill was moving closer to the door. 'Three years?' she breathed.

'Honey, these feelings will get better with time. You won't ever forget, and some days will be sadder than others, but I promise you, you can learn to live with this. You just need to take it one day at a time. You just need to breathe.'

She could feel empathy pouring out of her as she tried to reach out to the teenager behind the door. The teenager who thought that no one could understand.

The voice was quiet—almost a whisper. 'It would have been my dad's birthday today. He would have been forty-five.' Kristie's heart twisted in her chest. Of course. A birthday for someone who'd been lost. The roughest of days.

She heard the strangled sob again. All she wanted to do was put her arms around this hurting young girl. 'I get it,' she said steadily. 'Birthdays are always hard. I'm not going to lie to you. I've cried every birthday, Thanksgiving and Christmas that my sister hasn't been here.' She took a deep breath. 'Just know that you're not alone, Jill. Other people have gone through this. They understand. You just need to find someone to listen. Someone you feel as if you can talk to. Do you have someone like that?'

The reply was hesitant. 'It should be my mum. But I can't. I can't talk to her because she's so upset herself. She cries when she thinks I can't hear.' There was another quiet noise. Kristie recognised it. Jill had sat down on the opposite side of the door from her. It gave her a sense of hope.

'Okay, I get it. What about if we find someone who is just for you? Someone you can talk to whenever you need to?'

'Th-that might be okay… But…'

'But?' prompted Kristie.

'I don't want to have to go somewhere. To see someone.'

'Would you talk to someone on the phone? Have you tried any of the emotional support helplines around here?'

'M-maybe.'

Kristie sucked in her breath. 'Did you talk?'

There was silence for a few seconds. 'No.'

Tears were brimming in Kristie's eyes.

'I… I just wasn't ready.'

Kristie rested her head on her knees. One of the things that Rhuaridh had said before clicked into place in her mind. About all you can do is the best that you can. She wiped her tears again. 'Are you ready now?' she asked.

'I... I think so...'

'Jill, can I come in?'

There was the longest silence. Then a click at the door. Kristie cast a glance over her shoulder to where the teacher and Rhuaridh were standing. Her heart twisted in her chest. He hadn't believed in her. And for a few seconds it had felt like a betrayal—like the bottom had fallen out of her world. But she would deal with that later. Right now, she was going to do the best that she could.

'Kristie...' The voice came from behind her.

But she just shook her head, opened the door and closed it behind her.

He sat there for hours. First talking to the teacher, then to Jill's frantic mother, who'd practically run all the way from the ferry. He'd managed to get hold of a children's mental health nurse who would come and see Jill tomorrow from the mainland. This wasn't something that could be fixed overnight.

Kristie finally emerged from the classroom

with her arm around Jill's shoulder. Jill threw herself into her mother's arms and Kristie waited to talk to both mother and daughter together. Just like he would expect a professional counsellor to do.

She'd been a star today. And he knew she'd been scared. He knew she'd had to expose part of herself to connect with the teenager. And words couldn't describe how proud he was of her right now.

He stood to the side until he was sure she had finished talking, then joined her to let Jill and her mother know the plans for the next day.

The rest of the students had now been sent home so the school was quiet, silence echoing around them. Rhuaridh lifted his hand to touch Kristie's cheek. 'I can't believe you did that,' he said quietly.

She met his gaze. 'I had to. She needed someone to talk to—someone to listen—and I could be that person.'

'I'm so proud of you. I know this must have been difficult.'

Something jolted in his heart. He hadn't wanted to say these words here, but he had to go with the feelings that were overwhelming him. 'I love you, Kristie. I've spent the last few months loving you and was just waiting for the right time to tell you.' He held up one hand, 'And even though it's a completely ridiculous and totally unromantic place, the right time is now.'

He couldn't stop talking. 'And I know it's ridiculous because we live on different continents and both have jobs and careers. I don't expect you to pack up and live here. In fact, the last thing I'd want is for you to come here and resent me for asking you to. But I had to tell you. I had to tell you that I love you and you've stolen a piece of my heart.' He lifted his hand to his chest.

She blinked and he could see the hesitation on her lips and his heart twisted inside his chest. He'd taken her by surprise. She hadn't been expecting this.

For a few seconds she said nothing. He'd said too much.

All his insecurities from Zoe's desertion flooded back into his brain as if he'd just flicked a switch. Her look of disdain and disapproval. Kristie's face didn't look like that—hers was a mixture of panic and…disappointment? She was disappointed he'd told her he loved her?

He was a fool. He should never have said anything. He'd just been overwhelmed with how proud he was of her that he'd obviously stepped across a whole host of boundaries he hadn't realised were there.

There was a laugh beside them and he pulled his hand back sharply.

'Oh, the Hot Highland Doc. I'd heard you were in the school.'

Rhuaridh turned to the teacher who'd just walked up beside them. 'What?'

The teacher just kept smiling. 'The kids talk about you all the time.'

He shook his head, thinking he hadn't heard correctly. 'What did you call me?'

'The Hot Highland Doc. It's a great title, isn't it? Better than the Conscientious Curator or the Star-struck Astronaut. Pity the geography is off.'

She gave a shrug and kept walking on down the corridor.

Rhuaridh tried to process the words. He spun back to face Kristie. 'She's joking, right?'

Kristie looked a little sheepish. 'I… I didn't

have any say in it.' They were the first words she'd said since he'd told her he loved her.

He stepped back and looked down at himself. 'Hot Highland Doc? That's how you've described me to the world? Of all the ridiculous descriptions...' He shook his head again. 'And we're nowhere near the Highlands!'

He was overreacting. He knew that. But right now he felt like a fool.

A few things clicked in his brain, comments he'd heard people say but hadn't really picked up on at the time. 'I can't believe you'd let them do that.' Then something else crossed his mind. 'I can't believe you didn't warn me.'

Kristie breathed. The air was stuck somewhere in her throat. He'd just told her he loved her, then almost snatched it back by inferring they could never work. It was like giving her a giant heart-shaped balloon then popping it with a giant pin.

Her stomach was in knots. For a few seconds there she'd thought the world was perfect and their stars had aligned, but then Rhuaridh had kept talking. Was he talking himself out of having a relationship with her? Had she only been pleasant company while the filming was going on?

It was as if every defence automatically sprang into place. 'It's not up to me to tell you. The TV series hasn't exactly been a secret. Most of the island watches it. If you weren't such a social media recluse you would have picked up on it in the first month.'

Her brain was jumbled right now. Everything felt so muddled.

'Was any of this real for you? You tell me you love me one second, then tell me how ridiculous our relationship is in the next? Who does that? What kind of a person does that sort of thing?' The words were just spilling out in anger. No real thought because all she could feel right now was pain. All the things she'd considered for a half a second seemed futile now. Coming to Arran? Accepting the book deal and giving up the TV job? How on earth could she leave LA? She was crazy for even considering anything like that.

There was a flash of hurt in his eyes then his jaw clenched.

The anger kept building in her chest, turning into hot tears spilling down her cheeks.

She stepped back and looked him straight in the eye. Her words were tight. 'And...we're done. Goodbye, Rhuaridh.' She had to get out of there. She had to get out of there now.

Her pink coat spun out as she turned around and strode down the corridor. Her heart squeezed tight in her chest, part hurt, part anger. Why on earth had she thought for even a second that this might work?

He watched her pink coat retreating, trying to work out what the hell had just happened. He'd told her he loved her and she'd walked away.

There was a movement at the end of the corridor. A camera. Thea.

It appeared he'd just been starring in his own worse nightmare.

Fury gripped his chest. He put his hands on his hips for a few seconds, staring down as he took a few deep breaths.

This had all been for nothing. He'd been crazy to think they could ever make this work.

Then he straightened his back and walked in the opposite direction.

CHAPTER TWELVE

April

'I QUIT.'

'You can't quit. The show has just been syndicated.'

'For once, Louie, listen to what I tell you. I quit. I'm not setting foot on that island again.'

'Your contract says you are.'

'So sue me.'

Kristie slammed the phone down just as it buzzed. She turned it over.

Can we talk?

She stared at the name. Rhuaridh. Her hand started to shake.

NO.

She typed it in capital letters.

* * *

Last time he'd been this tired he'd been a junior doctor on a twenty-four-hour shift. He'd been delayed at both Glasgow then London airports. The heat hit him as soon as he set foot on the tarmac in Los Angeles. Most people in the UK drove cars with gears. Rhuaridh had never driven an automatic and hadn't quite realised it almost drove himself, meaning when he put the car into reverse in the car park at the airport, he almost took out the row of cars behind him.

He was torn between trusting the air-conditioning and just putting down the window to let some air into the car. It was dry. Scratchy dry.

He hadn't slept a wink on the flights. He'd been too busy thinking about the way they'd left things. Once he'd calmed down he'd tried to find her, but it seemed that she and Thea had caught the first ferry off the island.

He'd spent a few days replaying everything in his head. Trying to work out why things had gone so wrong.

Rhuaridh didn't want to call. He hadn't really wanted to text either, he just wanted to see her. He wanted to be in the same room as her. He wanted to talk to her.

He'd only sent the text once he'd landed, when he'd had a crazy second of doubt that he'd look like some kind of madman turning up at her door uninvited.

His brain wobbled at the number of lanes on the highway. At this rate he'd be lucky to make it there at all. Being called the Hot Highland Doc at least a dozen times between Arran and Los Angeles now seemed like some kind of weird irony. For the first time in his life complete strangers had recognised him. He'd been asked for autographs and selfies. People had asked him to speak so they could hear his accent. And there had been lots of questions about Kristie.

Most people had been completely complimentary—but he was sure that was because there was a lag time of six weeks between filming and the finished episode being shown. Once they saw the next episode that was scheduled—which would surely contain their fight and Kristie walking away—he was pretty sure he'd be toast the world over.

But here was the thing. He wasn't worried

about the rest of the world. He was only worried about her.

He pulled up outside an apartment complex in the Woodland Hills area of Los Angeles. It looked smart. Safe.

He lifted his chin and pushed every doubt away. It was time. Time to put his heart on the line and tell this woman—again—just how much he loved her. Just how much he was prepared to do to make things work between them. She might still hate him but he had to try. And he could only try his best.

There was a rumble outside her apartment door, followed by a buzz. Was she expecting a delivery? She didn't think so.

Kristie looked down. She'd been wearing this pink slouchy top and grey yoga pants for the last two days. She hadn't even opened the blinds these last few days. She was officially a slob. She shrugged and headed to the door, pulling it open to let the bright Los Angeles sunshine stream into her apartment.

She squinted. Looked. And looked again. Her breath strangled somewhere inside her. Was she finally so miserable that she was seeing things?

'Hey.' The Scottish lilt was strong. She couldn't be imagining this. 'I thought we should talk.'

Her hand went automatically to her hair, scrunched up in a dubious ponytail. She didn't have a scrap of makeup on her face. Every imaginary meeting between them she'd had in her mind these last few days had been nothing like this.

'Can I come in?' She blinked and looked behind him. Three large cases.

'What are you doing?'

'I'm…visiting,' he said cautiously.

She automatically stepped back. 'I just texted you.'

'I know.' He smiled.

She shook her head. 'I said I didn't want to talk.'

'And if you don't then I'll leave,' he said steadily. 'But I've flown five thousand miles. Can we have five minutes?'

She gestured to her sofa. 'Five minutes.' She moved quickly, picking up the empty wrappers from the cookies and chips that were lying on the coffee table.

Rhuaridh sat down heavily. He'd flown five thousand miles to talk to her.

Her brain was spinning.

She'd replayed their last moments over and over in her head. She'd always known he'd object to the title of the show—*she'd* even objected to it when she'd initially heard it. But because he didn't go on social media, or the streaming network, she'd always secretly hoped he wouldn't find out. She'd been lucky. Up until last week. And the timing had been awful because by that point she'd felt so hurt and angry that she hadn't felt like explaining—hadn't felt like defending the show.

'How's Jill?' she asked.

He nodded. He was wearing jeans and a pale blue shirt that were distinctly rumpled. He gave her a thoughtful smile. 'It's baby steps. And everyone knows that. But she said I could let you know how she's doing. She's seen the CAMHS nurse and a counsellor. Two days ago she told me that she'd phoned the number in the middle of the night when her head was spinning, she couldn't get back to sleep and she'd felt so alone. She told me she'd cried, and that the woman at the end of the phone had spoken softly to her until she'd fallen asleep again.'

Tears pricked at Kristie's eyes. 'It sounds like it's a start.'

'Everything has to start somewhere,' he replied. It was the way he said those words, the tone, that made her turn to face him. 'And so do we.'

He sighed and ran his fingers through his hair. 'Kristie, I'm sorry, I feel as if this all spun out of control and I still can't really work out why. Except...' he paused for a second '... I probably put my foot in my mouth.' He didn't wait for her to reply before he continued. 'The one thing that I know, and I know with all my heart, is that I love you, Kristie. I don't want to be without you. And I don't care where we are together, just as long as we get a chance to see if this will work.'

His words made her catch her breath.

He kept talking. 'I hated how we left things.' He shook his head. 'I hate that we fought over... nothing. I love you. I can't bear it when you're sad. I can't bear it when you're feeling down. I just want to wrap my arms around you and stop it all.' He gave a wry laugh, 'And, yes, I know it's ridiculous. I know it's probably really old-fashioned.' He put his hand on his chest. 'But I can't help how I feel in here.'

He took a breath. 'When I told you that I loved you and you didn't reply, I made a whole host of assumptions. Then my mouth started talking and my brain didn't know how to stop it. I thought it was crazy to dare to hope we could be together. It's what I wanted, but how selfish would I be to ask you to pack up your whole life for me? To move from your home, and your career, to be with a guy you'd spent a few days a month with?

'So...' he gestured towards the cases '...because I'm so hopeless with words I decided to try something different.'

She stared at him, her voice stuck somewhere in her throat.

'So...' he paused and she could tell he was nervous '... I decided that actions speak louder than words. That's why I've packed everything up. Magda is due back at work and we've got a locum for the next few months.' He shook his head. 'The irony of doing the show is that we had about twenty people apply. So...' he met her gaze '...if you're willing to talk, if you're willing to give things a try, just tell me. Tell me where your next job is, and this time I'll come to you. Because I love you, Kristie. I'll love you to the ends of this earth.'

She stared at him. Trying to take in his words. 'You'd move here? To be with me?'

'Of course. I'd do anything for you, Kristie—whatever it takes.'

She sagged back a little further into the sofa, then turned her head to face him. His words were swimming around her brain—the enormity of them. Her heart was swelling inside her chest. Those tiny fragments of doubt that had dashed through her mind when he'd made the suggestions about moving had evaporated. She raised one eyebrow, curiously. 'What makes you think I don't like Arran?'

He shot her a suspicious glance and counted off on his fingers. 'Er…maybe the weather. The ferries. Or lack of them. No supermarkets, no malls.'

She leaned towards him. 'Maybe I like all that. Maybe I like waking up in a place where the view changes daily. Maybe I like a place where most people know each other's names.'

He sat forward. It was obviously not what he was expecting to hear and she could see the hopeful glint in his eyes. 'Can I have more than five minutes?' he whispered.

She licked her lips and took a breath. If this was real, if she wanted this to be real, she had to be truthful—she had to put all her cards on the table.

'I've been angry these last few days. Angry with myself and angry with you. When I came to Arran I wanted to tell you that I loved you too. And when you told me first, then added about how it was all crazy and we could never work…it was like giving me part of my dream then stealing it all away again.'

He grimaced.

'I wanted you to ask, Rhuaridh. I wanted you to do exactly what you're here to do now, for me, without the big gesture. All I wanted you to do was to ask me to stay. To ask me to choose you, and to choose Arran.'

He blinked, a mixture of confusion and relief sweeping over his face. 'I thought that would be selfish. Conceited even, to ask you to give everything up.'

'Just like what you've done for me now?' She held her hands out toward his cases.

He let out a wry laugh and shook his head,

reaching over to intertwine his fingers with hers. 'It seems that we both crossed our wires when we were really heading for parallel paths.'

She gave a slow nod of her head. 'I want you to know that I've made a decision.'

He straightened a little. 'What kind of decision?'

'A take-a-chance-on-everything life, love, career decision.'

He opened his mouth to speak but she held up her hand. 'I love you, Rhuaridh. The whole world could see it before I could. I started to dream about getting on that ferry, reaching Arran and never leaving again. I've started to like rain. And I definitely love snow. And my job?' She pulled a face and held up her hands. 'It used to be everything, but it's not been that for a long time. Not since Jess died. My family died. Not since I started volunteering at the helpline.' She looked at him nervously. 'I've had enough of TV. No matter what they offer me right now, the only offer I'm going to take is the book deal.'

'You have a book deal?' His eyes widened. 'That's brilliant!'

She looked up into his eyes. 'You gave me the

push I needed, you made me write the book in my heart. And you were right. There's been a bidding war. The publishers love it.'

He stopped for a second and tilted his head. 'Is that the only offer you're going to take?'

She licked her lips. 'That depends.'

'Depends on what?' He'd shifted forward, it was like he was hanging on her every word. Funny, handsome, grumpy, loyal Rhuaridh— her own Scotsman—was hanging on her words.

'I came to Arran to tell you I wanted to stay.' She rested her hand against her heart. 'That I'd lived my last few months in Technicolor. It was the life I'd always wanted. I'd found a man I loved and a place I thought I could call home.' She shook her head. 'I know the title of the show is ridiculous. Of course it's ridiculous. It's a TV show. But honestly? At the time I didn't think it was worth the fight. And...' she pressed her lips together for a second '... I honestly hoped you wouldn't find out.'

He reached over and touched her face. 'Kristie, I don't care about the TV show. I love you. I flew all this way to tell you that. Please forgive me. I'll move anywhere in the world with you. But if Arran's where you want to be, then nothing would make me happier.' The glint appeared in his eyes again. 'Mac will never forgive me if I don't bring you home. He hasn't looked at me since you left.'

She smiled. 'Mac is missing me?'

'He's pining. Like only an old sheepdog can. The only look he gives me these days is one of disgust.'

She edged a little closer. 'Well, when you put it like that, I don't want to see Mac suffer.'

His arms slid around her waist as her hands rested on his shoulders. 'I mean, every dog should have two parents.' Her hands moved up into his hair.

His lips brushed the side of her ear. 'I absolutely agree.' He looked at the three large suitcases at the doorway. 'Now, are you going to help me get those cases home?'

EPILOGUE

One year later

THE BRIDE'S THREE-QUARTER-LENGTH dress rippled in the breeze as she walked towards him clutching orange gerberas in one hand and Mac's lead in the other.

It felt as if the whole island had turned up for this event. The local hotel had hired three separate marquees to keep up with the numbers but whilst the sun was shining they'd decided to get married outside so everyone could see.

Rhuaridh's heart swelled in his chest. Kristie's hair wasn't quite so blonde now, her skin not quite so tanned, but he'd never seen anything more beautiful than his bride. Her grin was plastered from one side of her face to the other.

He leaned over, winking at Gerry, who sat on a chair nearby holding a camera, capturing the ceremony for them, then turned back and held out his hands towards his bride's. 'Now, no fancy moves, no running out on me.'

Her eyes sparkled. 'We're on an island. There's nowhere to go and...' she winked '... I'm not that good a swimmer. I guess you'll have to keep me.'

He slid his arms around her waist. 'Oh, I think I can do that.'

He bent towards her as Gerry shouted, 'Hey! Wait up! It's too early for a kiss.'

The celebrant laughed as Kristie slid her hands around his neck. 'What do you think?' she whispered, her lips brushing against his skin and her blue eyes continuing to sparkle.

Mac let out an approving bark and the whole congregation laughed too.

'Oh, it's never too early for a kiss,' said Rhuaridh, as he tipped his bride back and kissed her while the whole island watched.

* * * * *